Why I Loved You

I Wanted to Fly

POOJA SHARMA

Order this book online at www.trafford.com
or email orders@trafford.com

Most Trafford titles are also available at major online book retailers.

Printed in the United States of America.

ISBN: 978-1-4669-7010-6 (sc)
ISBN: 978-1-4669-7008-3 (hc)
ISBN: 978-1-4669-7009-0 (e)

Library of Congress Control Number: 2012922127

Trafford rev. 11/21/2012

 www.trafford.com

North America & international
toll-free: 1 888 232 4444 (USA & Canada)
phone: 250 383 6864 ♦ fax: 812 355 4082

I would like to express my gratitude to God for making it possible to complete my novel. Thanks to my family and all those who supported me in the tenure of writing and special thanks for all the people who are going to show their trust on me by purchasing the copy of this novel.

Chapter 1

August 2007.

"*Yes*, one day, I'd also fly," Rose vowed while nodding at the snug cerulean blazer of the air hostess. The gleam of the airlines had always been enthralling for Rose since her childhood. And today was the day she's travelling to find the path to enter into the flying career.

Life brought the dream in factual after a long, strenuous struggle. She had finally secured a place at the Aviation College of New York. She was elated and started packing luggage and shopping for her new destiny at New York. Since childhood, she had dreamed of a career in aviation, thinking probably she may get the chance in acting.

Rose's parents and elder sister came to drop her at the hostel. Though she's occupied with joy, her family burst into tears as this was the first time they would leave their daughter alone. Rose didn't cry for a minute. She unpacked her baggage and initially shared the room with two other girls.

On July 2007, first day of her aviation class, Rose was too delighted to dress up in the aviation uniform: squat azure skirt and light-purple shirt with a scarf. In the afternoon, at twelve, class started, and the aviation teacher appealing Rose that she dreamed herself one day flying in the air and be like her. The first lecture was over, and the outcomes of the first day were how to dress and basic grooming etiquettes. After long hours of classes, Rose returned to the hostel and had lunch unaided, sitting in the hostel canteen, watching a crowd of around eighty girls from different backgrounds and nationalities.

At midnight, she had the opportunity to talk with her other roommates. One was from Rose Aviation Academy, and the other one was her senior at Aviation College. Confab went on the entire night, and all three girls exchanged their backgrounds. They found each other quite similar in their dreams but Rose; she was different from these girls. She had a beautiful heart-shaped face, was tall like a model at 5.10 feet, had a fair complexion, and had flawless and glowing skin.

She distinguished herself from other fellow roommates and her aviation pals. Out of the batch of sixty students, she was the most charming and deserving to reach the helm of the aviation industry. After some days of unvarying classes, Rose discovered New York to be a place of dreams. Life here was full of fun and joy. The former months of classes were quite dreary. She used to call her best friend Celelia, a classmate from junior college. They discussed for hours and hours, and this way, she managed to pass her time in the evening. One month passed in the new city, and Rose enjoyed life to the fullest.

One day, after coming from class, Rose found a new friend named Christina; she was her adjoining neighbor in the hostel and batch mate. Gently, Rose and Christina were mounting a rational understanding. Fairly after one month of companionship, they started going to class together, frequently hanging out, and doing regular shopping also.

Some days later, they shifted in the same room, leaving their previous ones. Rose's routine completely relied on top of Celestina. She woke up late in the afternoon whereas Christina woke up regularly and drove to the canteen in the morning to take breakfast. To fetch the breakfast for Rose was a part of Celestina's routine now. Celestina would leave it on the desk for Rose when she woke up. Soon after, they would get ready for classes.

Fascination to attend classes didn't last for long. For a couple of weeks, it was a gratifying experience in the classes; later on, it was wearisome to attend regularly. Soon, they bunked their classes and explored the city of their dream destination: New York. Just in a fortnight, they managed to visit all the famous places of the New York. By this time, it was over a fortnight last they haven't attended the classes. Subsequently, they got a call from their tutor for not attending the lectures regularly. To avoid any future niggling, they decided to attend it for a week, and after marking the attendance, they vanished again.

The beautiful bond of friendship had crossed one month. Christina wasn't a career-oriented girl. Consequently, she continued to spend most of her time in chatting with and dating boys. Opposite to Rose and Christina's hostel, there was a boys' hostel too, which was clearly visible from their room windows. Its gigantic build accommodated around a quarter of hustlers.

At midnight, Christina normally opened the window facing the boys' hostel. She deliberately changed her clothes whenever boys were standing in front of their building. Rose wasn't cognizant of her best friend's infuriating conduct. After a long time of undertaking, Christina was caught by the hostel vendor and was given a warning to vacate the hostel. Rose was ignorant until this time. She got ready to evacuate the hostel for her best friend, and just in a few days, they managed to get the two new sitting rooms in the same area.

"Why did you change rooms?" Rose's mom questioned.

"Oh well, Mom, the food wasn't as good as compared to other hostels," Rose betrayed.

"Oh my, honey, it's okay. Do inform us before you make any decisions in the future."

Her parents were quite tranquil and blissful for their daughter. Rose was enjoying it here at its fullest and sometimes attended the classes too. She was hastily accustomed to the new place and found it more comfortable than the preceding one. After a fortnight in this hostel, one day, while coming back from classes, she got a call from the hostel manager.

"Why do you glare out of the window of your room and give indications to the boys?" the manager yelled.

"Pardon." Rose went to the room without replying further.

Celestina was also accompanying Rose when she went upstairs. Celestina replied, "Yeah . . . please pardon me this time. I'll not reprise it again," Christina pleaded.

Not only this, she occasionally changed her clothes, going naked to seduce boys in front of their building facing their window. Rose didn't recognize anything until now; she was amazed at her manager's statement. Replying nothing, she went to her room and was worried a lot about this state. All this happened today when Christina didn't attend classes, excusing herself. "I'm not well."

Rose trusted her best friend Christina and shared all the words with her. Rose's problem wasn't over. It seemed to be worsening when her hostel manager took out the registration form of Rose and called her home the very next day and articulated the entire story to her mother. In addition, "Your daughter has to evacuate the hostel," the manager said explicitly to Mom.

"Why? What are you talking about?" Mom groaned.

"Whatever you hear," the manager said tediously.

Rose accredited all this when she was in her classes and her mother called her,

"What are you doing there? Come back home. Did I send you there to embarrass us?" Mom screamed.

She scolded her without allowing Rose to utter a single word. Rose was throbbed with the thought of leaving the city. She, indeed, wasn't feeling well. Instantly she returned to the room and searched for the manager who inquired for Rose.

"I'm sorry to bother you," the manager apologized.

Before Rose could say anything to him, he amazed Rose. *What's the new drama?* she wondered. She came to clarify that she hadn't done anything. Later, she went to him to clarify the matter.

"How did you come to know all that?" Rose inquired.

"Rose, one of your neighbors has told me the truth. In your absence, Christina used to do all those things."

She wasn't creating all that drama, but her roommate and chum, Christina, was responsible for all this.

"But how can you say that?" Rose probed.

"The girl's name is Laura. She witnessed Christina undertaking all this. And also she portrayed your innocence," the manager explicated.

Rose serenely strode toward Laura's room. They were acquainted to each other since Rose came to this hostel. Laura was in the same batch of aviation classes in which Rose and Christina were.

There was a new friend emerging into Rose's life that supported her and exposed the truth to the manager. Today, both grabbed dinner together and started sharing and discussing about their individual lives.

"Hi, thanks for the favor," Rose said, gratified.

"Hey, never mind," Laura countered.

"Well, I'm from the Virginia, pleased to meet you."

"Aha. That's such a coincidence. I'm also from the same city."

"Lovely, isn't it?"

It was implausible for Rose that Laura also belonged to the same city where she came from. She lived in the same area adjacent to the Rose's residence and accomplished college from the same college where Rose did.

Both were amazed to discern about each other. Just a day gone and they decided to shift in the same room. Rose took all her possessions to Laura's room. They started going to their classes together, evading Christina in the hostel and at classes. Laura and Rose were of the same height and the same figure, but Laura was fairer than Rose. Laura's communication was feeble. Rose assisted her in assignments, and Laura took care of her food and other routine things.

They found good company in each other and regularly went out for shopping, lunch, and dinner. If one wasn't in the hostel, they waited until the other came. In this way, both were pleased for a few starting days. Rose and Laura were single until this time and virgins too. Though Laura had many friends and practiced chatting on the phone regularly at night with them, Rose passed her night by standing by the window or listening to soft music.

Their class time was just for three hours as they were pursuing the diploma course after secondary college. Laura thought to take an admission parallel to a bachelor in business administration (i.e., BBA) so that she can gain a bachelor's degree simultaneously. Both became chums shortly.

Succeeding Laura, Rose also took the admission in the same course, but they continued doing the aviation course in New York and graduated at their hometown, a beautiful place in the United States. Soon after this, they started going to the coaching nearby their hostel early in the morning. Laura was prompt and disciplined; daily she got up early in the morning and made breakfast for Rose as she woke up late. Laura started waking up, her earliest at 7:45 a.m., and Rose woke up only after ten. Because of this, she always missed her morning tuition. Things were going right for Rose and Laura for now.

One day, soon after their afternoon aviation class, they planned to go to the beachside just to chill out. They dressed up quite seductively and seemed to be alone without boys. When they reached their destination, they tried some new flavors of cocktails and some nonalcoholic drinks, resting in beach dresses and enjoying the sunlight there.

At six o'clock, they recalled to go back to the hostel as the timing allowed until 9:00 p.m. only for getting an entry in the hostel. After a wonderful time at the seaside, they started packing up and looking out for the taxi to drop them fast. After a long wait for an hour, they got a private taxi. On the way, suddenly they realized that one car was uninterruptedly following them.

"Are those guys following us?" Rose probed.

"They must be going the same way," Laura assured.

After covering half of the distance, they realized that they were truly chasing them since the beach. The driver took notice and informed the girls. The taxi driver wanted to stop the car and inquire the folks.

"What do they want?" He murmured.

"Don't know," Rose and Laura said in chorus.

"Please don't stop the car," Laura entreated.

The driver conceded and continued to drive. Some miles after, they tried to overtake their car and started tendering the glass of the cab. However, the chivalrous driver acted heroically and didn't frighten up. He continued to drive until they reached their destination. Waiting for the girls to move out of the car and see them.

"Thank God!" Rose and Laura sighed.

They quickly made the payment to the driver and entered into the hostel room. Both discovered an immense peace in lying down in bed after a terrible drive. While changing their clothes in the dark and desolate, loud voices started peeping in Rose's head when she stood to undress.

"Laura, Laura, wake up. Please wake up!"

"What happened, Rose?"

"Can you hear some noise coming from the road? Seems like some group of people are standing on the road and shouting at us."

"Hey, look at that. They're still standing?"

Laura switched on the light, stepped close to the window, slightly opened the curtain, and looked down.

"Oh! Rose, they're the same guys who followed us from the beach. They're standing downstairs and shouting for us to come out," Laura whispered.

"Let's be quiet and don't reply anything. Just close the door and the curtain and let's sleep before the hostel warden comes to know about it," Rose said. Both went to sleep.

At 9:00 a.m., Rose and Laura came down from the third floor and rushed to college. They noticed that last night's boys carved on the walls of their building. Laura noticed a mobile number and a note: "Hey, pink girl, this is for you. If you like me, then call me."

Without giving it much importance, they left for their classes and tried to forget the incident. Today it was their aviation classes six months over and they had some specified assignment.

"Oops, we forgot to buy stationery for the assignments," Laura recalled.

"Let's go then before the market shuts down," Rose alleged.

At 6:00 p.m., while returning from the shopping and after taking dinner outside, a few minutes away from the hostel, they detected a Land Rover following them again. They were on foot. Hastily they strode off without turning around.

"Give me your contact numbers," a stranger roared.

Coldly they ran toward the hostel and safely reached their room. They were stunned for a few moments, resting on the bed.

"Yeah, they were the identical guys who followed us yesterday from the beach," Rose screamed.

"Yes, they were."

"How to get rid of them? They know our address, and we don't even know their names."

"I think they're behind you, Rose!"

"What?"

"I guess they're following you."

"Eh, why me? You were also with me that day."

"But you were wearing the color pink."

"Yeah. Don't scare me."

"I'm not. Maybe one of them seriously loves you."

"Hmmm . . ."

It's not easy to survive in the luxurious and incredible city of New York without any steady earnings. Mounting overheads and seclusion awaken Rose. Her monthly expenses continued to increase when she came in the company of Laura. Thousand-dollar pocket money isn't ample for Rose for her living expenses and maintenance, whereas her chum procures twice of Rose's pocket money.

Dearth of money and a lot of spare time aroused Rose to get a job. After Laura moved out regularly to encounter her boyfriend at daytime, she felt bored and found it difficult to pass the entire day alone. This was her third month running outside home. Her job hunt had begun now.

On Sunday afternoon, Rose was lolling in the hostel canteen unaided for lunch when she found a group of girls chatting about some part-time job opportunities at Citi Financial. The work was for backend position underneath the relationship manager.

Rose overheard all their conversation and went down to her room. She didn't know any of the girls; however, she was desperate to have a word with them.

At the beautiful dusk, while Rose's mind was juggling with ways to search out the job, she found her chum chatting to same girl whom Rose observed discussing about some part-time job. Unpredictably, she was Laura friend.

She brought her friend into their room and shared all the details about the job to Rose. The information gathered by Rose restored her liveliness, and the hopes to continue in this city once gain fluttered in her mind. The night was filled with the thought to fly high in the sky. Rose joyfully started preparing for a next-day interview for her first job.

On September 1 at 9:00 a.m., Rose woke up early, imagining what to wear for her interview. Filled with excitement, she prepared to dress up pleasantly and professionally. However, she didn't know what to do as this was her first interview for a career in a multinational brand like Citi Financial.

After a three long hours, finally, she dressed up in indigo trousers, a purple shirt, with an open hairs just one single band, and black high heels, prepared for the interview.

The interview venue was very close to Rose's hostel, so she reached it on foot.

"Excuse me, can you please tell me where the relationship manager's cabin is?" Rose asked the receptionist.

"Ma'am, please wait for a few minutes."

Rose was anxious but occupied with her dreams. The office ambience was pleasant enough, and she affectionately fell in love with the company. She desperately desired to grab an opportunity to work here. A few minutes later, a middle-aged pygmy man clad in a cobalt shirt and dark trousers, with black curled hair, a fair complexion, and wearing specs, wended from the front office.

Rose couldn't hold her gaze to stare at him. First expression makes her fancying of him and thought, *Oh, God, please send him in my life.*

Up to now, Rose hadn't dated any person moreover hasn't accompanied with any male friends. This was her first time to get in contact with any male.

Later on. "Ma'am, you may please walk into the cabin."

"Thanks!"

Miraculously, Rose was in front of same person whom she pleaded to come into her life. The interviewer, Edward Lewis, designated as relationship manager at CITI Financial, probed with conventional questions, likewise brief introduction about herself, convenient timing.

"I want a break of three hours for my aviation classes," she said, seeking permission.

"Sure, no problem," Edward Lewis said as he formally granted and offered her a part-time job as backend support and asked her to join starting the next day.

"Sure, sir. I'll be here tomorrow."

September 2, 2007 at 9:00 a.m.

"What to wear for the first day at the office?" Rose asked Laura.

"Well, wear our aviation formal attire or else go for semiformals."

Rose was getting ready for her first day in the office. Laura brought breakfast from the canteen for her. After one hour of debate about dressing, Rose left for the office. To her amazement, her manager was already there and engaged with his work.

Rose knocked. "Please may I come in, sir?"

"Yes, please. Please be seated."

While Edward was busy with his calls with the clients, Rose keenly observed him to be assigned some tasks. At 12:00 p.m., Rose was still waiting, but the manger was dealing with his clients and was in some meeting now. He arrived in the cabin for ten minutes; Rose hesitantly asked for the break to attend her classes.

"Sure, you may leave."

She acquired permission and rushed for the hostel. Laura was keenly waiting for her with lunch. She undressed the formal clothes and wore the attire, took some curries, and recklessly attended classes.

It was going to complete the first module of her diploma, so they had some assignments due by the middle of the current month.

Yet again, in a hurry, she reached the hostel and changed for the office. Edward Lewis wasn't present now. Subsequently, she had no other option but to wait unaccompanied in the cabin. After a long wait, at dusk, Edward peeped in.

"That's it for today. We will carry on tomorrow, and I hope to see you on time."

"Sure, sir," said Rose, ashamed.

Soon after she stepped back into the hostel, shockingly, she couldn't find Laura there. First, she thought to relax after coming from the hectic schedule; later on, she intended to call Laura. It took long for Rose. At nine o'clock, the kitchen and main entrance were about to close, and Laura still had not arrived. She started calling Laura; however, the phone was out of network.

She kept the phone and started making dinner for them both. Up to now, they had never taken dinner without each other. The whiff of delicious lox and bagels drives tempting. She couldn't hold it anymore after a starving day. She again tried calling, but there was no response, profoundly waiting for her to come and share the office incidents.

She tried to pass time standing at the window. Latterly, Rose noticed the chatter coming from the ground floor. "Whatever, let it be," she shrugged off. A few minutes after, she scrutinized that the manager was quarrelling with some couple. When she perceived prudently, "Oh, this is Laura arguing with the manager," she whispered and immediately descended to the entrance.

She noted that Laura was fighting with the hotel manager to get entry into the hostel. In addition, entry was only allowed for the hostel female students.

"Sir, please, this is the first time, and I assure you it will never happen again."

"Okay. Today I'm letting you, but next time, I won't allow it," the manager warned.

Thankful, both came safely into their room. However, Rose was astonished and filled with lots of questions.

"Where were you? Why did you come too late? Is he the same beach guy?"

"Wait . . . wait . . . let me explicate. But first, take some foodstuff. I brought dinner for you."

"I'll take it afterwards. First, reply to me."

"Okay! Today, when you went to the office early in the morning, I received a text from Jacob to meet him just once. After that, he'll never trouble us," Laura explicated.

"OMG!"

"Initially, I wasn't engrossed to go, but later on, I believed I had better go and get rid of this person. When we came back from classes and you left for the office, again he texted me, saying, 'I'll pick you from the hostel and drop you as well.'"

I said, "Okay."

At four o'clock, he came to pick me up and entreated, "Please close your eyes, I wanna give you a surprise."

"Yeah," I agreed.

Jacob stopped the car after forty minutes, took me outside the car, walked for a while, and then removed my eye cover slowly . . .

"A beautiful scene, no one around except us at the dusky sequestered place in front of me. The sky was full of clouds. Jacob emanated from behind me, and gradually, he came beside me, his hands around my waist. He walked closer to the edge of the road, leaning downward to the ditch, and reverberated, 'I love you, Laura.'"

"How romantic. Then?"

"I love you a lot." Bended on the knee, holding a red rose, inarticulate, "I want to spend my whole life with you. Will you?"

I was gasping. I felt anxious, and I happily replied yes.

"That's too romantic. What happened after that?" Rose probed.

We strolled to a luxurious five-star hotel. Jacob was exultant for proposing to me, and my approval has given him a new course of life.

"This is the most delightful day of my life. You've made my life complete. Thanks for being in my life. Will you do me one more favor?" Jacob demanded.

"Yes," I said.

"I'll take dinner, if you'll feed me from your hands," Jacob added.

"Yeah . . ." I was dumbstruck at this and didn't know what to say. This was the first time in my life I felt the existence of my spouse. After we completed dinner, Jacob offered me this ring, but I denied because I wanted to wear it in front of the family. He agreed. On the way, we stopped. I thought you must have been waiting for me for dinner, so I ordered for you as well. Because of this, we got late.

"Oh, I see, you're fortunate to find out your soul mate." Rose applauded.

"Anyways, how was your first day at the office?" Laura asked.

"Hey, first, many congratulations for being in a relationship. My day was good. Today, my boss was engaged with work, so he didn't get time to elucidate me." Rose exhaled.

Two quarters of the year had elapsed slickly. Rose had congregated expedient aviation-sector awareness alongside the financial sector. However, right from the first day, she had fancied her boss, but she never expressed anything during office hours. Whenever she got time, Rose perceived out what other affiliates were doing.

"Socialize with the staff and make networking with the other people and talk something to me as well," Edward counseled.

"Sure, sir. I'll follow this from now onwards," Rose responded.

"Rose, tomorrow, in the morning, I've to visit the other branches, so you can also go there directly in the morning, if this is feasible for you?"

"But, sir, I don't have any convenience to go to that branch as I'm living in a hostel, and I don't own any vehicle," Rose revealed.

"Okay, never mind. I'll pick you up from your hostel. Get ready at nine a.m."

"Sure, sir."

On September 15, 2007, Edward reached Rose's hostel at 9:00 a.m. sharp. Rose alighted wearing some decent casuals. Edward deeply kept his eyes on her dress but couldn't utter a word. Gingerly, she got in the car.

"Good morning, sir!"

"Lovely morning to you," Edward welcomed.

"Would you be comfortable if I'll drive above 100 km/s as we're getting late?"

"Yes, I don't mind."

"Let's speed then."

The entire day was hectic for both, and they couldn't avail the opportunity to chat with each other. However, Rose was free in the midst of some hours.

In the evening time, while returning from the office, after being occupied the entire day at the new branch, Edward suddenly realized the muteness in the car and couldn't hold it in anymore but asked Rose, "Why don't you speak anything?"

"What? I mean, what should I say?"

"Whatever you like. Apart from your professional life."

"Hmm . . . there is nothing as such—"

"I can say one thing: either you treat me as your brother or as your friend, whichever you're comfortable with. At least you'll communicate something," Edward suggested.

Rose, after thinking for a while, said, "So what do you want to hear, friend?"

"Okay, that sounds better. So tell me how many people you have in your family, and what's their occupation?"

"Father is a government employee. He's working in the accounts department. Mother works as a primary teacher near home, and sister is just pursuing her physiotherapist," Rose answered.

"I also have a nuclear family like you."

Rose's life was moving smoothly. She was pioneering in her tasks and professionally gaining good international exposure. Her very first job was a brand like Citi Financial—a multinational corporation. Moreover, she was accompanied by her worthy chum Laura as well. Life seemed to be comfy at this moment. On the contrary, her best friend's life was also going well. She was enjoying her first love relation. It was going to be a fortnight at Citi Financial, and Rose was still unaware of her job outlines.

On September 20, Rose was working in the office and doing some data-entry work assigned by the manager when she heard rumors going around her office about her dressing, as she dressed up in casual sleeveless tops and loose hair.

After some time, Edward also entered the office and heard a bit of these rumors prevailing in the office. He had a close colleague, and he instantly convened with one of the staff members. "What's going on in the office?"

"Yeah, don't know, sir."

"Please don't be scared. I won't disclose this to anyone."

"Sir, Rose isn't coming in the attire since last week."

As she's from the aviation background and has a seductive, sexy personality like models. The crux of the nattering in the office was Rose's attire. For all the bachelors of this branch, Rose was their daily dose for their eye toning, and for girls, she was a matter of envy.

Momentarily, Edward took action.

"Dear, it's an office. From next week onward, please come in formals, and if possible, tie your hair also. As you can understand, I'm responsible for your reporting, and I need to proceed the report further to the top level, so I don't want any problems in future. Hope you can understand," Edward asked graciously.

"Sure, sir. I'll go and shop. From next week onward, I'll be in formals."

"Thanks! This is it for today. Will meet you on Monday then."

"Where're you now?" Laura rang her.

"I'm just leaving from the office."

"I and Jacob are waiting for you. Come to the ice cream parlor near our hostel."

"Okay, I'll be there in a few minutes."

"Hi, Rose, this is Jacob. You know him, the love of my life, and, Jacob, this is my chum Rose," Laura introduced them to each other.

"Rose, lovely to meet you. Just now, we were discussing about you. Anyways, tell me, how's your job going on?" Jacob questioned.

"It's good. I'm learning a lot. You say how your life is."

"All fine, dear. I'm extremely cheerful nowadays because of your best friend."

"Well, I know that."

Laura so shall we order now. "Rose, what will you take?"

"I'll just have the vanilla flavor."

Jacob ordered the ice creams for all, including his friends also.

"I'm planning to go out to the seaside point. Girls, will you be ready for that?'

"But we need to the reach hostel at ten p.m.," Rose and Laura said in chorus.

"Don't worry about that. We'll return after an hour and we'll drop you there," Jacob assured.

This was the first meeting of Rose, Laura, and Jacob. All became genial in the first gathering. As this was the first time all the people gathered, it took them a long time to return. All of them were lost so much that no one evoked the time, and they finally reached at 10:00 p.m.

As expected by Rose, the hostel manager had closed the entrance and wasn't ready to take the girls inside. Jacob was watching from inside the car, and the girls were banging at the door, but didn't get any response from the manager.

"I think he'll not open this way. Let me rap out. You people wait. Till the time he opens the gate we'll not go," Jacob said, suggesting the solution.

"Hey, manager, can't you hear. Open the gates. Otherwise, we won't let you sleep. Come outside, come outside."

Lights on. Someone from the hostel reception was opening the door. Laura and Rose requested Jacob, "Please don't say anything to him when he comes out because he may complaint at home."

"Sure. As you people wish."

"Let him come, and we'll see," Jacob whispered.

All the boys came out of the Jeep, waiting outside the doors for the manager. All eyes on the doors muddled when they noticed a short-statured, slim boy was coming out with the keys. Without saying anything, he opened the door.

"Could you please enter your names in the register and then move to your rooms."

All were relaxed now and calmly moved back. Jacob called Laura's phone, "Is everything all right?"

"Yes . . . hope so. We don't know who this new guy is. We saw him for the first time."

"If someone says anything to you people, then let me know."

"Yeah, sure," Laura replied and kept the phone.

Nowadays, Rose's routine had changed as she would go to the office on time, and after that, she would directly join Jacob and Laura. They would wait for her at the ice cream parlor or at some restaurants. It had been a long time that both haven't taken their dinner at the hostel. Watching Laura and her partner, Rose also desired for the love mate to share her life with him.

One day, while returning from the office Rose,

"I've also complete my work, and I'm moving towards your hostel, so if you don't mind, can I drop you there?" Edward offered.

"Okay," Rose agreed, and without having much conversation, she reached the hostel. As Rose entered the room, Laura prompted, "So, madam, what's the scene?"

"What?" Rose yelled.

"What's going on these days? What are you hiding from us?" Laura taunted.

"Oh . . . nothing's like that. Why I'll hide with you? As such I don't have anything to hide," Rose clarified.

"Okay, never mind. If you've something in mind or in life, do share with me all."

"Yes, sure. Why not? Who else can I share with?"

Chapter 2

Professional life seemed to be paramount for Rose. She was attaining experience, what she wanted for her career, and relished working under a multinational corporation. It was time for their class submission as some of their assignments were due. It was late at night when they prelude their submission because Rose emanates late from the office, and until that time, Laura spent time with Jacob at his flat. At night, by nine o'clock, both realized that tomorrow was their submission, and they weren't equipped with the stationery.

"We'll be requiring some plain papers and colored glitter pen to make this project," Rose recalled.

"I've an idea. I'll say to Jacob he'll bring all these, but the problem is how he'll hand over to us, as the hostel will close at nine?"

"Let me descend and talk to the new supervisor of the hostel as he can collect all this and can give it to us."

"Hope so this would work. You go down, and I will try to connect to Jacob."

At 9:00 a.m., Rose and Laura still strained to finish their assignments. After a long, tiring night, Rose got ready for the office, and Laura was completing the assignments for both.

Rose arrived at the office late again. Edward scolded her for repeating the same thing.

"Sir, I had the submission today, so I got late," Rose explicated.

"Okay, no problem. If you want, you can go and complete it first, and you can come back," Edward said.

Rose was delighted. *What could be better than this?* she said to herself and went back to the hostel and helped Laura. They managed to finish it before classes and went back after submitting. Rose arrived at the office,

"Thanks for the favor, sir!"

"How was your assignment?" Edward asked.

"It was excellent, and thanks, sir, for allotting me the time," said Rose appreciatively.

Edward assigned her some work and left for the office visit of their branches in New York. Rose completed the work early in the evening and was winding off when Edward suddenly stopped her.

"I'll drop you at the hostel." In the car Edward inquired about the work she'd completed and learned.

"Sir, I've completed the data entries of this month for our HNI clients," Rose responded.

"So how's everyone in your family?"

"Sir, all are fit and fine." Rose's hostel arrived and conversation interrupted in the mid.

She got off the car and then moved slightly to the restaurant to meet Jacob and Laura. By 1:00 a.m., Rose was ready to sleep after a delicious dinner with her friends, changing her nightgown and putting the lights off. Surprisingly, she noticed a call from an unknown number. First, she didn't pick up. Incidentally, it might have been a wrong number, and she was feeling too sleepy as well.

She ignored it and left the cell ringing and went under the blanket.

At 1:30 a.m., again she received a call from the same number. Sluggishly, she picked up the mobile in her hand and watched it cautiously, but after few seconds, the moment the phone was about to get disconnected, she received the call again.

Rose, taciturnity for a while, waiting for the person to say something. Suddenly, she heard a male voice.

"Hi, Rose."

She could certainly recognize this voice and woke up happily after hearing it.

"Hi," she tried to pretend that she couldn't recognize the voice. She was having a hint of this voice but wanted to check. "Yes, who's this?"

"Is this Rose?"

"Yes, this is Rose speaking. May I know who's this speaking?" she examined graciously.

"This is Edward Lewis speaking."

"Yes, sir," Rose said charmingly.

"Hope I'm not disturbing you, dear."

"No . . . no . . . Not at all, sir."

"So what's up now?"

"Nothing, I just ended chitchat with the roommate."

Edward was a bit shy and nervous and wanted to talk to Rose more but didn't know how to start and what to say.

"Okay. Actually, I called you to let you know that tomorrow I won't be coming to the office. Officially, I'm visiting a New York suburb, so if you don't want to come, then you can also take off."

"Sure, sir, I'll let you know in the morning."

"Rest is okay with you?"

Rose, tickled and happy inside, replied, "Yes, sir, all fine."

"Okay then. Good night and take care. Let me know in case you need some help!"

"Sure, sir."

Edward kept the phone and went to sleep. Rose was flabbergasted to receive a call from the boss and was beaming for no reason at night. Witnessing this, Laura, who was in bed next to Rose's bed, probed her, "What happened? Suddenly, you woke up."

"Nothing much. I'm not feeling sleepy," Rose lied.

Laura woke up and disconnected her phone chat with her boyfriend, and both started chatting to each other. Mutely, they ascended to the roof of the hostel. Laura suspected Rose about the phone call because, so far, she was single and didn't have any boyfriends to talk to or any close friends. As for her routine, she got to bed before 1:00 a.m. and woke up late in the morning.

She didn't prompt her cagey about the matter to Rose but was waiting for her to explicit. For the first time, they were at this plafond and enjoyed the night to its fullest; otherwise, on usual days, Rose slept at this time, and Laura discussed on the phone with her boyfriend, Jacob.

Night seemed to be noble for these people. Fancying love and to get settle in love life this year only.

"How does it feel to be in love?" Rose was curious to know from Laura as she'd never been in any kind of relationship before. Besides, Laura being lot many times before. She was occupied with many queries to ask Laura, but she probably couldn't ask all her personal questions openly.

"It can't be defined—how it feels to be in a relationship—but can be felt. Still at present, I feel like my life is complete. The existence of one person is sufficient enough to live an entire life, and the absence of that same person feels like the entire world is missing," Laura expressed.

Rose kept on querying on the same topic, pause from Laura's side. She was surprised to listen to all this kinds of questions from Rose as she'd never discussed this matter before.

"What happened to you, darling? Today you're so much nosy to know about love. Is everything all right with you?"

Laura got a bit of a clue about Rose's life. She perhaps had an idea of what Rose felt but didn't disclose it in front of her at this time. Their conversation lasted until late that night. It's morning at 4:00 a.m., and they had office at nine; however, at this time also, they were lively to exchange views about love and did not feel sleepy.

"Rose, it's too late now. Better to go for a sleep. Otherwise, we won't be able to wake up on time," Laura recommended. Rose wanted to carry on the discussion, but she stifled spirit about loves.

At 10:00 a.m., both were sleeping until it was late, unaware that they needed to go to office and college. Almost half of the hostel had left for their work and office, and these people were still dreaming.

Knock knock.

The cleaning staff was here to clean all the rooms. They found Rose's room open, liberally entered the room, and started cleaning. A few minutes later, Laura noticed the Hoover sound. Shocked, she glared at the cleaning maid. "What's the time?"

"Ten thirty a.m.," informed the staff member.

"Wake up . . . wake up, Rose. We're too late for work . . . Get ready soon!" Laura yelled.

"What happened? Why are you yelling in my ears? Let me continue with quiet slumber."

"You're late for the office. It's half past ten now."

Rose, amazed at seeing the time, hastily got ready for work, and Laura got ready for college. Rose didn't take a bath. Whenever she got late, she did this. Without taking breakfast, Rose left for the office, wondering, *What to excuse the boss for coming late?*

She worked out an ample number of excuses for her late arrival. At last, she thought to say, "My roommate wasn't well, so I took her to the hospital." *If Edward will ask me, then I'll answer this*, she thought, desiring that Edward might also get late.

Scarily working on excuses, she reached the office afraid to face her manager. Calmly and politely she asked, "Please, may I come in, sir?" Edward gesticulated for her to sit at her place as he was occupied with his work and on chat with his senior manager.

Anxiously, Rose inchoately worked, keen for the boss to communicate about the arrival. Later on, Edward got a call from the receptionist that some of his clients were waiting to meet him. Without wasting a single minute, Edward got up and buzzed off to the meeting room. Rose was lolling in her chair as her work was finished; her mind was stoked with the morning incident, and every moment, fear of the scolding kept her uneasy.

She was jaded as she was inactive in the cabin, viewing out the window. She couldn't stop her gaze on her boss, keenly observing all the actions of Edward: the way he talked and dressed up, his professional skills, and many more.

It was lunchtime. Half of the office had gone off their desks to take lunch. However, Rose was sitting bare stomach, starving and bothered about their classes. It was the first time she was in the office at lunchtime, still waiting for the manger to come and seek his permission either to leave for classes or for lunch as she hadn't taken anything since the morning. Relaxing in the chair, scrutiny the Edward to get free and talk with him, seek permission to leave for the classes.

Edward was occupied with his clients, and after handling the morning clients, his junior came to discuss further about the targets. Again, he acquired with his junior, who was also a close colleague of his.

At 2:00 p.m., lunchtime ended, and Edward left to visit the other branches of New York. Rose was still in the cabin, waiting for him to come, but the afternoon also seemed to be bad like the morning was for Rose. No task to perform, stomach calls for the input, she missed today's lecture too, and this morning's incident is yet to be conversed. It was a long day for her to pass, deprived of work and food.

She tried to socialize with the office staff in the absence of Edward as he stated earlier to make networking. This time, it didn't work as all the people were busy in achieving their targets and completing their routine work, unlike Rose who was only appointed to assist Edward.

Her tolerance to bear the hunger was over. Rose thought to leave the office, but then she gave a thought it won't be a good idea to leave without informing the manager. Perhaps he may get heated.

At 7:00 p.m., Rose wind of her work, started packing her bag, and was about to leave the office. Suddenly, she noticed Edward was entering the office from her cabin. She stopped for a while and again sat on the chair.

He'd definitely talk about the morning incident, Rose uttered in her mind. This thought made her panic, and she continued to sit mutely.

"How was your day?" Edward questioned.

Rose was stunned to hear this as she was expecting something else, but softly and precisely, she replied, "Fine." She wanted to leave hurriedly from the office and to take some food. However, Edward was in a mood to dialogue with her.

"I apologize! That today I wasn't able to allocate you some work, and you waited for the whole day. I hope you must have gone for your classes on time," Edward inquired.

"Actually, sir, today I missed it because I thought it'd not be a good idea to go without your permission," Rose replied serenely.

"Oh . . . oh . . . I'm extremely regretful for this. I'll make sure this thing won't happen next time. Actually, today I got stuck with the work, so I didn't even have time to take lunch even."

"That's okay, sir . . ."

"So that's it for today. You must be starving. If you want, I can drop you at the hostel," Edward offered.

After a few minutes' silence, Rose said, "Well, if you don't have any problem, then I won't mind."

Gingerly, they stepped out from the office. Rose was standing at the parking, waiting for Edward to come. Timidly, Edward drove the car to the Rose's room. He was so desperate to talk to Rose but shy to express and ask about last night's phone conversation. Somehow, he gathered courage, and after driving few miles, he inquired, "Hope so, I didn't disturb you yesterday night?"

"No, sir . . ." Rose chuckled.

"You don't talk much. Is this since childhood, or are you not comfortable with me?"

"Nothing like that, sir . . . perhaps not getting words to express . . ."

"What *nothing like that*? It's been a long time now, but you never talk to me much. Am I too boring?"

"Aaahh . . . sir, actually, yesterday I was surrounded with my roommates, so I couldn't talk to you much, and ordinarily, you're so busy, and I'm also occupied at office hours. Maybe because of that."

"That's okay . . . here's your hostel," Edward parked the car in front of the hostel entrance.

Rose was waiting for Edward to open the car gate, but he didn't open it for a minute. Rose was overlapping her fingers, eager to enter the hostel and get some food, but it seemed like Edward had got some different mood. Rose was perceiving the hostel as the security guard had noticed the presence of someone inside the car, and some of her hostel pals were also standing outside.

Two minutes later. "Sir, can you please open the door?"

"No . . ."

"What?"

"No . . . I said no clearly," Edward replied assuredly.

"Sir, lemme go. Folks are observing me."

"If you don't mind and if you'll allow me, then can I compensate your lunch today?" Edward invited.

"Sir, I don't get you."

"I meant to say because of me, you missed lunch today, so can I take you for dinner tonight? Right now . . ."

"No, sir, it's already too late, and I can't get entry after nine here. Sir, not today. Probably next time."

"Please . . . please . . ." Edward insisted, but Rose denied.

"As you wish, dear, I don't want to force you. I'll wait," Edward said, agitated, and Rose, after greeting good-bye, entered the hostel.

As soon as she arrived, she noticed Laura and her other roommate, Linda, giggling and peeving at her. Both were trying to escape her and simply chuckling. Rose dodged their eyes and went inside the bathroom to change her clothes. She wanted to discern their weird behavior. "What happened?"

Laura and Linda didn't utter anything and started giggling for no reason. "What happened to you girls? Share with me also so that I can also laugh."

"Let it be. Don't say anything," Rose urged.

"I can't wait anymore, and I haven't taken anything since morning." Rose countered.

"I haven't taken dinner, but I took lunch with Jacob. I was waiting for you only. Let's go upstairs without delaying anymore. Otherwise, the canteen will close," Laura responded.

They hastily moved upstairs for the dinner. Suddenly, in the midst of it, Laura says, "Have you seriously not taken anything since morning?"

"Why? What happened? I told you before. Why are you asking repeatedly?"

"Don't be annoyed. When you were entering the hostel, Linda saw you getting off the car, so I thought you must have gone out with someone. Just like that. Nothing much," Laura revealed tranquilly.

"*Oh* . . . Now I get the point why you people were simply chuckling when I came inside the room. Yeah . . . actually, the entire day, I wasn't having any work to do, and I couldn't go to classes because my boss was absent at the branch."

"Oops."

"It wasn't a good idea to go without the permission of my boss. As far as coming from the car is concerned, the boss came out the same time as I, and he passes from this way only, so he dropped me, and you people have made simply big gossip."

"Okay! I got the point. Forget it, and have a dinner. You must be very hungry, and don't mind for that," said Laura remorsefully.

Rose felt much better now. They descended to the room; Laura got on the phone with her boyfriend, and Linda was cramming for her exams.

Whenever Rose didn't have anything to do or she wasn't feeling drowsy, she simply stood by the room window, facing the road. However, a new thought popped into her mind. She had aspired for the flying career, and being in the part of glamour world for which the flying carrier is the step to it. Instead, today, she was fancying for marriage. Her recent gatherings have replaced her dreams for flying.

The sequestered and deserted night, by twelve, was interrupted with the jangling from Rose's side. Linda went to sleep, and Laura was lying in bed, ongoing with her phone chat with Jacob. Suddenly, Laura and Linda were startled and scrutinized Rose's bed. Rose vigilantly dashed toward her bed.

She was embarrassed for the disturbance created in the room because of her, jumbled what to excuse these people, she grinned them and wafted out of the room, discarding mates wondering.

Chapter 3

Edward (***Citi Financial***) calling.

In the murky darkness, Rose moved to the secluded plafond of the hostel. Nothing can be seen except the sky. Tenderly, she picked the phone but till the time Rose reached at the top, it got disconnected after the complete bell rang. Edward disconnected the call.

She pondered for a moment, profoundly waiting for the bell to ring again. Although for two minutes, the phone didn't ring. Chaotic, nervy but happy, she wanted to talk to him but didn't have daring to call him, discerning as he's the manager on one side and on other side she fears that he must have recalled the morning incidence.

Rose picked up a beautiful red rose behind her and started tearing it. "To call or not to call." enduring it till the last petal. Almost reaching the last, surprisingly, she grasped the phone and saw "Text from Edward." Hurriedly, she opened it: "If you're free, then give me a missed call?"

Rose, without waiting a mo., called back.

"Yaa . . ."

"How are you?"

"I'm good . . ."

"Why are you breathing so high? Are you out somewhere?"

"Actually, I came to the rooftop."

"Just called you up as full day we're with the work and wanted to apologize once again for today."

"No . . . no . . . Sir, that's okay. It's fine." Rose was dumbstruck and relaxed after the connectivity.

"So you pardon me or not?"

"Yes, sir. In fact, I wasn't angry with you . . ."

"Thank God! My good luck. I was wondering about the same as I went back home. I thought I'd talk to you tomorrow in the office, but you know very well we're busy at the office and barely get a chance to talk."

"Yaa . . . I can understand. No problem."

"So our dinner is due. When are you going to give me the pleasure to dine with you?" "Aaahh . . . Aaahh . . . I can't say anything right now. Probably soon."

"I'm desperately waiting for that day . . ."

"Yeah . . . Sure, sir."

Both wished to talk more but didn't know how to begin the conversation. Edward probed some common questions only, and Rose answered him as usual, not putting anything from her side.

The frigidity of midnight at 2:00 a.m. and the cold wind of the open uncomforted Rose. Edward was also exhausted and felt drowsy. Their chat lasted for around two hours. They desired to talk further, but their weary bodies weren't allowing them to do so. Edward delicately requested, "Okay, dear. Allow me to put down the phone, and we'll continue to chat later. It's too late now as you must also be feeling sleepy."

"Hmm . . . no problem. Sweet dreams."

She descended to the room and furtively opened the gate so that nobody noticed her. While Rose was shutting the door, to her astonishment, Laura was still awake. She rotated her head and detected her, but she didn't say anything so that she didn't feel awkward. She switched off the lights and surreptitiously lay down in the bed.

Leisurely turning in bed but not getting sleep, her mind was still reeling about the phone chat. She was grinning for no reason, and her eyes were open, trying to fall asleep, but after finding it hard to get forcibly she closes her eyes, wrapped in blanket, spread it above her head and pushing her to sleep.

Next morning, she woke up early, choosing what to wear as if she wasn't going to the office but to a casual meeting. Today, she had chosen to dress in casuals than in formal wear. She put on her rosy shirt, revealing her cleavage, with her snug indigo denims. Edward wondered to see her before time as none of the staff members arrived yet; merely cleaning staff were vacuuming the office. Receptions was empty; she was simply roving in the office and looking out for the Edward to come by the window. Progressively, staff members started arriving one by one. It was 10:00 a.m.; Rose couldn't catch Edward in his cabin.

She approached the front office. "What time is Mr. Lewis going to come?"

"Sorry, ma'am, I've no clue about it."

Desolately, Rose returned from there and went inside the cabin to complete the pending task. Time was running deliberately today. To solace herself every moment, she pore out from the window to watch if the presence of Edward's car was parked out or not, but to her melancholy, the car wasn't there. It was now going to be lunchtime when she received a call from the Edward.

"I'd arrived at the office in the late evening as my elder manager was arriving to visit the other New York branches, so I'm accompanying him. If you want to leave now, you can leave and come back in the evening."

Rose left for her aviation classes. In all her afternoon lectures, she was inattentive as her mind was waiting for the evening and going back to the office. The new module initiated on grooming ethics, and she was not very interested to assemble there, stranded at the moment as she couldn't leave the lecture in between, and Laura was also with her, so she couldn't give any excuse.

At half past three, Rose and Laura returned from classes. "Do you want to join us for lunch if you're not going to the office?" Laura questioned.

Rose found it better to sit in the hostel alone rather than to go out for the lunch.

After coming back to the office, she was glad to see Edward in the cabin, mutely grinning inside to look at Edward. He saw her and in the first instance said, "Today you're looking beautiful compared to ordinary days."

Rose perhaps was wising for his admiration. "Thanks, sir."

Rose arose in a mood to work, but Edward asked her, "So can we go for our due dinner tonight?" After a minute pause. "But, sir, before nine p.m., I've to be in the hostel."

"Don't worry. I'll drop you before that," Edward assured.

He took her to a luxurious five-star hotel in New York and asked for her preference for dinner. Rose glimpsed at the menu.

"Sir, you say what's your choice and then I'll order. How can I order of my choice for you also?"

"Order whatever you like. I'll take from that."

"As you wish, sir."

"Why do you always call me *sir*? I'm not that much older than you. Please, you can call me by my name when we aren't in the office," Edward elucidated.

"Okay, I will next time."

"No. Why next time? Try now." Edward insisted.

After denying for three or four times, Rose addressed Edward by his name. Meanwhile, their order was ready to be served. Rose ordered the chicken biryani with champagne for Edward and fruit wine for her. "Rose, I'm amazed that you don't take alcohol." More than surprised, he was glad for this.

"Sir, there's nothing to be astonished about . . . oops . . . I mean, Edward, there's nothing to shocked about. I just don't sense the requisite of alcohol," Rose countered.

"Well! That's good for your health, and maybe I guess it'll be good for your prospective husband as well."

Both were almost about to finish dinner. All of a sudden, Rose reminded him of the time. Swiftly they finished the dinner. Like a gentleman, Edward paid for it. Warily, Rose sat in the car, sitting mutely. Edward was waiting for her to communicate, but as always, he was only going to start.

"I hope you enjoyed the dinner with me?" Edward said, trying to continue some conversation as Rose never started any talk.

"Yaa, it was good, and I enjoyed your company too." Rose giggled.

They were going in a compact mini Vauxhall car. Edward figured it out—Rose wasn't relaxed as she was sitting, sticking to the door, and placing her hands adjacent to her body, legs overlapping each other.

Viewing this, he wondered, *Oh god! My car is small but I brought it for me only. Never thought someone else would accompany me, but what should I tell her now?* His mind was muddled as he wanted to ask her to be calm. Instead, he remain hushed.

It was time to say good-bye! Edward conveyed Rose to the hostel ten minutes before the ending time. He saw her off and paused there until Rose entered the hostel.

After seeing her on the second floor from her room's window, he left for his home. Laura and Linda were revising for their exams although both gave a nasty smile at Rose as she entered the room. Rose cringed, as she hadn't noticed anything, and jolted, changing her clothes. Later on, "Laura, have you taken dinner?" Rose enquired.

"No . . . you forgot we dine together regularly." Laura grimaced.

"Well then, quickly get up. We need to go up, otherwise, the canteen will be closed."

They ascended upstairs and took dinner as usual days. Rose didn't divulge to Laura that she had already taken dinner and pretended to accompany Laura as naturally as before. Laura detected that Rose wasn't eating properly and simply sat munching deliberately unlike the usual days.

She suspected her but didn't utter anything. Likewise, after some time, Rose requested Laura to have more, but she denied. She also ate little compared to ordinary days. Rose was also dubious of her, but she also persisted in being discreet and pretended to eat.

Both insisted that the other eat appropriately, but they weren't in the condition to eat further as they had already taken dinner, but just for the sake of companionship, they came here.

Chapter 4

August 31, 2007.

Every progressive day carried a resonant change in Rose's life. Late-night phone talks were a quantum of Rose's routine. She had moderately established with the beliefs and civilization of this revered city. Cognitive enough from the city financial, she was on the edge to complete a quarter in this company. Edward had vindicated spanking manager for her until now. She had also magnificently accomplished six months of her aviation classes and had started working for the career seminars and conceiving for the interviews. They have been attending the airline interviews frequently. The entire day, Rose worked at the office while at night she got occupied on the phone, chatting with her manager.

Rose was exultant today. Her efforts had paid off. She got her first salary of two months together; that was a thousand dollars.

"Hey, time to celebrate. When are you planning to give me a party?" Edward craved.

"Anytime, sir," Rose said generously.

Edward and Rose buzzed off to a trifling cafeteria and spent some eminent time. While they were rejoicing, they forgot the hostel deadline. Speedily he drove off to the hostel. At 10:00 p.m.,

Edward parked at hostel facade and remained hidden; by the time they see off, they came in senses of the hostel manager. Swiftly Rose got off from the car,

"Is there anyone? Open the gate." She pressed the button, but initially, for two or three minutes, no one noticed. Edward was still there, waiting for her to enter.

Rose started screaming through the holes of the gates and pressing the lock of the gate—no answer. Probably, it was going to be hard for Rose. After few minutes' struggle, she was a bit tranquil to perceive that a scruffy aged man with an angry expression on his face had opened the light of the hostel reception.

Coming closer to the gate, but relaxation didn't last long as this was idem manager with whom she had the argument for Laura's late arrival. Today she was caught.

"I'm not going to open the gate till you make your parents call me and justify," the hostel manager stated.

Rose was vexed as her parents were ignorant about this, and she couldn't call them. Otherwise, she wondered, listening to this, whether they'd probably call her back to her hometown and scold her. She was in a quandary because if she will not enter, then she'd also be in trouble. If the hostel authorities would notice that one girl hadn't put an entry in the hostel system, then the succeeding day, these people would notify her family. Rose didn't want this. Neither these people weren't ready to open the gate nor could she go anywhere else.

All of a sudden, Edward called Rose. "What happened? Can I go there and speak to your manager?"

"No . . . No . . . He'll aggravate," Rose murmured.

"What's he saying? Why isn't he allowing you?"

"He's asking to call my parents and wants to talk to them."

"Oops . . . Leave the hostel and accompany me in my home, and I'll drop you back in the morning."

"I need to go inside and make the entry in the system. Otherwise, they'll take the house landline number from my admission form and will say the whole story at home."

"Well! Do one thing—give them my mobile number, and I'll talk with him, imitating your father. Don't worry, it's going to work," Edward recommended.

Rose adored the idea, and she deceived the manager as if she was calling her father and asking him to talk to the hostel manager. She called from the manager's mobile to Edward's, acting like she was calling her father and handed it over to the manager when she got connected to him,

"Hello, sir, this's a call from the NY Moore hostel. Your daughter has ruined the rules of the hostel, and she came from outside after the deadline," the manager screeched.

"Sir, I apologize on her behalf. I assure you this thing won't repeat in the future. Please, I request you to allow her to enter the gate. As you can understand, at midnight, she can't go anywhere," Edward said as Rose's father.

"Sir, I'm allowing her on your commitment," manager urged.

Edward frolic abruptly to take Rose out of the problem. Now she was safely inside the hostel. She was happy since this morning, and again, she has got a new reason to develop esteem for Edward as he stood up for her.

Soothingly she entered the room, and it was quiet there as Linda went to sleep and Laura was with her studies. Laura was waiting for her to come and share some good news. Without changing her clothes, Rose prepared herself to face the interrogations of Laura, which she has already anticipated on the way.

"How was your day? Where were you till this time?" Laura delved.

"I had a splendid day! Today I got my first salary, so my manager requested me to give him a party."

"Lovely. When are you planning to celebrate with me?"

"No problem. We can go out tomorrow when I return from the office. You can ask Jacob also to join us."

"Well, that sounds good. I'm waiting for that. We'll enjoy tomorrow."

Next day, soon after office hours, Rose was ready to accompany Jacob and Laura. They decided to dine in a contemporary restaurant near their hostel. It was an excellent opportunity to win each other's heart. Rose ordered nonveg for her and Jacob, but Laura was a vegan in this group, so she ordered some veg fried rice and some veggie snacks for her. All were in a party mood today; Jacob wanted to tease his girlfriend, with Rose on his side, for being a veggie.

"Hey, this veggie item's trash." Jacob tormented.

"Yeah, I don't like veggie people. I don't know what they find in this," Rose goaded.

They did their best to annoy Laura, but she didn't get heated. Jacob came up with the notion to take Rose on his side, for convincing Laura eats non veg today. Rose alleged for a moment and said, "It won't be good as she has never taken nonveg. Probably, she'll feel bad if we will amend her veg food to nonveg."

"Oh come on, just for fun. Nothing wrong in that," Jacob disagreed with Rose, copiously in a mood to tease Laura.

"We'll just do it once. We'll change her curry with our nonveg one. Let me see whether she likes it or not. If she doesn't like it, then we'll never force her, but if she eats it, then our idea succeeds," Jacob said, coaxing Rose.

The waiter carried the dinner and was ready to serve the three of them, but cleverly, Jacob succeeded in implementing his tactics with the help of Rose.

Espionage Jacob and Rose underway their dinner, intensely inspecting Laura. She lifted up the plate and start pouring curry and rice into it. Both were frantically watching her; their plan was going to succeed soon as Laura had mixed the nonveg curry with the rice, supposing it to be veg. She was about to take the first bite. Rose wondered, *Should I stop her from eating this? I don't know, Lord. This'll be cheating on my chum Laura and supporting her boyfriend.*

Laura took the bite, and both were startled. Rose was a little edgy also about Laura's reaction when she would be cognizant of the nonveg. On the contrary, Jacob was glad. Both shushed and waited for Laura to consume the food. Laura finished the food and whispered, "I like the food. What about you people?"

"Yummy! It was delicious," Jacob and Rose chorused.

After spending a splendid time, they returned home. While on the way . . .

"Do we need to divulge the truth to Laura?"

"No . . . No way. It could hurt her," Rose contradicted. She wasn't in favor of this as she was scared to lose her chum. However, it wasn't going to halt Jacob's mood; he had primed up his mind to unveil the truth now.

"Hurray! You ate nonveg today. Vegan turned to nonveggie."

"No . . . no . . . How's this possible? I've never taken nonveg!" Laura replied furiously.

"Well, you can cross-check this with Rose."

"What's this Jacob said, Rose? Tell me the truth."

"Well . . . actually, Laura, in the restaurant, the curry which you ate was nonveg."

Jacob and Rose were expecting a fuming response from Laura. Rose envisaged, *Laura may spurt into tears and would definitely be exasperated with me.* Jacob wasn't worried but quietly thrilled to know how nonveg tasted.

"So you guys played a game with me and changed my food, but anyways, I liked that . . ."

Rose and Jacob guffawed.

"So you should be thankful to us that we made you eat the delicious?" Jacob goaded.

"Yes, I'm," Laura said mercifully.

After a delicious dinner, these people went back home and reached the hostel on time.

Rose and Laura were ready to get in bed after a draining day. With the lights off, all the roommates went to sleep, but Rose was still swaying in bed, not getting drowsy. She was contented for sundry reasons, but her mind was occupied in crafting romantic fantasies.

It was half past twelve, and now she was in the habit to sleep around half past two. She was indeed waiting for the call. Her mind wasn't allowing her to make a call to Edward, but her heart was constraining her to call. Shilly-shally went on until one at night. Her mind conquered her heart; she didn't call Edward, but he called her as always.

Chapter 5

On September 16, Rose was alone in the office, and Edward wasn't in the city. He went to New Jersey to visit the other branches that he lead. Rose found it dreary to work here unaided in the absence of her manager. She became hooked to his presence.

After returning from the boring and exhausting day, Rose apathetically went out with Laura for takeaway for dinner. She found it hard to spend her single moments.

Laura detected her behavior and inquired, "Hey, what's wrong with you?"

"Nothing much," Rose concealed.

Rose refused to converse anything about her feelings. Laura planned to go promenade or shopping, but Rose wasn't involved.

Forlornly, they returned to the hostel, and this was weird that Rose was hushed; she was entirely lost in her dreams. Routinely today also Laura served her with the dinner but she isn't intake much and impassive to eat and dialogue.

After having dinner, Rose mutely went to bed, simply lying down. She wasn't feeling sleepy early, but her mind was demanding and visualizing love dreams. Today, she went early, as she was aware that her manager was out of the town and working with another city branch. Consequently, she didn't expect a call from him.

At midnight, it was serene all around Rose, and all her roommates went to sleep while Rose, lost in the sleep, suddenly received an unanticipated call form the Edward. Promptly, she woke up and picked up the phone.

"What's up? What're you doing now?"

"Nothing much. I went to sleep."

"How was your day? Hope that I'm not disturbing you at this time?"

"Not at all, sir. My day was good."

"Anything new on your side? So when are you planning to get married?"

"What? What did you say?"

"Well, generally, I want to know, is there anyone you like or find right for marriage?"

"Yeah, I don't have anyone in my life," Rose said, tangled with what he actually wanted to know; however, she made it clear to him that she was single and never loved before.

"Really? A girl like you is still single? You're such a gorgeous girl, and then you haven't found anyone yet," Edward said, flabbergasted.

"Of course, you can say that I'm single, well, waiting for my perfect partner," Rose replied confidently.

"Hmm . . . if you don't mind, can I know what kind of guy you're looking for?" Edward fervently wanted to know about Rose's partner preference.

"Well, I haven't set some criteria's for the perfect person, but I'm just waiting for the right one." Rose cleared her thoughts.

"So can I ask you one thing about me? I mean, what do you feel for me?"

"Sorry! I didn't get what you mean?" Rose whispered innocently.

"I mean, what do you feel for me? As a person, am I good or not?"

"Yes, of course you're noble." Rose applauded.

"So do you like me or not?" Edward asked progressively.

"Yes, I do," Rose stated straightforwardly without waiting for the moment. Edward was explicit to Rose, and he expected the same from Rose.

"Please say something more," Edward entreated. The conversation reached its peak point. Today, after a long time of trials, it seemed like they had exchanged enough of their feelings. Nevertheless, the adage was missing. Edward found himself in an edgy situation as he cognized that Rose liked him, but he wondered, *If I'll say any further, whether she'd like it or she may probably leave the job.*

He didn't want so, call is still connected, and he wondered and amassed specific words to say to Rose. On the other side, Rose was intensely waiting for Edward's questions.

Edward paused and then queried, "Don't you want to ask me some questions about my personal life? If you've some interrogations, please ask. I'm ready to share with you." Edward craved.

"Well! When are you planning to settle down?"

"I'm ready to get married soon. Just waiting for the right one," Edward was jutting himself as the "single and ready to mingle" kind.

"That's lovely." Rose giggled.

"Rose, if you don't mind, I want to ask you something. Will you allow me?" Edward asked, seeking permission.

"Sure," Rose replied.

"Will you be my beloved?" Edward coyly proposed.

Rose was happy after her first love proposal. In fact, she was ready right from the first day, but she was introverted to say anything at the moment. She accumulated the words to express her feelings but was inept to say anything now however long she was waiting.

This was the first time someone had proposed to Rose. When she didn't reply for a few minutes, Edward got worried as he thought Rose crashed, so he tried to pursue her.

"What happened? If you don't like me, then no problem. I won't mind, but I request you not to leave the job. I'm truly sorry if I hurt you."

"No, Edward, nothing like that. I'm happy to listen to this. You needn't apologize!" Rose urged.

"Oops . . . You scared me. I thought I miffed you. If you aren't hurt, then reply to my question."

"Yes," Rose approved the proposal.

"What *yes*? What, should I consider this? I'm still unclear with your answer. Please elaborate and clarify." Edward was gratified and had a hint of Rose's answer but wanted to listen to the words straight from Rose.

"My answer is yes. That's all I can say as of now," Rose answered actively.

"Okay . . . It's too late now, and we need to go to the office early in the morning, and lastly, I love you so much. You also express it," Edward conveyed finally.

"Yes, me too." Rose loved him a lot and was ready to spend her complete life with him, but she was not comfortable to express anything on the phone.

It was two at night; Edward felt extremely blissful because he hadn't imagined a girl like Rose could come into his life. He was an introvert and was left with no other words to reveal his feelings. He assumed, *Rose's also shy, so it's better to talk one on one tomorrow.*

"See off, and we will meet tomorrow in the office."

"Okay." Rose didn't say bye or good night. She looks for the further talk.

"Dear, please say good night and bye so that I can keep the phone," Edward prompted.

"If I'll not say it then?" Rose wasn't ready to put down the phone.

"If you'll not say it, I won't keep the phone and morning we've office also, so please wish me soon *good night,* and *love you,*" Edward once again requested her.

After requesting twice, Rose agreed to keep the phone, though she was interested for more conversation. The chat went on until 4:00 a.m., and pooped Rose kept the phone and greeted him good morning now instead of good night.

On September 17, Rose woke up late as she slept in the morning. She hastened for the office.

"Good morning, darling! Join me for breakfast?" Laura offered.

"Thanks, dear! But I'm getting late for the office." Laura noticed a strange happiness or an unknown beam that she had never observed on Rose face formerly.

Laura was also concerned for Rose's temper last night. Consequently, she tried to chat and make her serene, but to her amazement, she's elated. Laura was trying to fathom it but couldn't.

At 11:00 p.m., Rose strode off to the office and pursued Edward. She was unable to see him from the main ingress as his car was parked beside the building. She dissolutely walked toward the reception and glimpsed Edward's cabin, but she couldn't notice him.

Covertly, she confirmed Edward's attendance from the front office and discerned his leave for today. Unobtrusively, she returned to the cabin and started working for the day. Startlingly, at lunchtime, when she was shutting down the systems and was about to leave for classes, she caught Edward standing behind her. She moved behind and sat on the chair.

"What happened? Did I scare you?" Edward asked.

"Yaa, sir," Rose said, upset.

"How's the work going on?"

"Progressing."

"So what are you planning now? Have you taken lunch?"

"Nothing. I just finished the work and am heading for classes."

Before Edward could inquire anything else, one of his juniors came in the cabin and asked for his assistance. Meanwhile, Rose sought for the break; she returned to the hostel and left for the classes.

Rose's daytime was virtuous today. They'd got the marks of the previous assignments, and she topped the class up to now. On the contrary, Laura was poor in her studies and English language. She only scored the passing marks. They came to know that probably in the next month, Delta Air Lines was going to conduct an interview at New York for the cabin crew.

All her batch mates were thrilled about the news, and for Rose, this was her childhood dream: to fly for Delta Air Lines and get entry into the glamorous Hollywood world. Opportunely, Rose returned to the office soon after classes. She was expecting the presence of her manager and wondering to share the news with Edward.

Edward wasn't in the branch. Rose endured with her work until evening, 7:00 p.m. Half of her colleagues left for home, but Rose was still at the office, not for work but for him. When she noticed the emptied office, she also planned to leave as it was almost night and most of the office lights were off. However, she accumulated courage and remained there at the cabin.

"If Edward won't arrive after ten minutes, then I'd also move out," she planned. She bleakly packed the work and picked her gloomy leather handbag. Suddenly, Edward entered the room in a hurry and took his seat. "So what now?"

"Sir, nothing much. I've completed the entries of this month and replied to all the customers." Rose giggled.

"What's the plan now?" Edward probed, relaxing in the chair.

"Well, just going home as usual." Rose desired to chat with him but was incapable of expressing herself.

Edward stood up from the chair, marched to Rose's side, gently held her hand, moved forward, and pushed her to sit in the chair. Appalled, she took the seat. Edward stood opposite to her chair against the table and yelled, "Why don't you want to talk or come with me? I asked you something yesterday, but you didn't say anything. We need to converse about our future."

Rose listened to him and felt reluctant as Edward was holding her hand. "I'm ready to chat and discuss," Rose replied steadily.

"Come. Sit in the car."

He was still holding her hand and drove her to the car. As a respect to his ladylove, he opened the door of the car. Rose obliged to this. He didn't notify her about where they were going. She was vexed and wanted to know where she was moving out, but Edward sustained the quietness and didn't disclose it till they reached a picturesque place outside the countryside. Rose was nosy to know where she was, but Edward wanted to surprise her.

After a long drive of thirty minutes, the car stopped in front of a beautiful four-star property outside the city area. Rose was visiting here for the first time. She was electrified to come here with her would-be partner. Rose was delighted to know that Edward had already booked a table for them and had planned a romantic dinner.

He pulled the chair for the Rose to sit; once again, Rose developed a soft spot for her manager, who was now partner for her. They seated, waiting for the dinner. While the dinner came, Edward devoured the time without wasting a single tick.

"I apologize if you're angry with me. I planned the dinner without your permission," Edward impulses.

"No problem. The place is good."

"I hope you aren't angry with me for my conduct in the evening," Edward interrogated.

"Of course not."

Edward had voluminous things to share with Rose. Unfortunately, they had limited time because of Rose's time restrictions. He started the evening conversation by sharing about his family background so that Rose would know all about his family.

"Well, how many people are there in your family?" Rose questioned.

Edward was pleased to hear attention from Rose for his lineage. "Well, my parents are divorced. I live with my mother and little sister, but I'm in touch with my father. He serves the ministry of the United States."

Rose was stunned to know his family status.

"I come from a political background. I've been raised by the maternal uncle's side. Soon after my mother divorced, I shifted with the grandfather. He lives in Texas. My maternal uncle is in the FBI at New Jersey and later one is in politics in New York," Edward added.

"OMG, that's good. You come from a wealthy background."

"Yes. My maternal aunt also serves in politics. Grandfather is the president in Texas, representing the Republicans. I'm his fondling grandson. He's also respectable for me."

Before he could express further, dinner was ready to be served. It was Rose's favorite chicken biryani and soup with the wine. This was another surprise for Rose's evening.

"How is the dinner?" Edward prompted.

"Lovely."

This was their first dinner after commitment. Both spent quality time with each other; the romantic dinner and chat made them forget all the worldly things. At nine o'clock, Rose reminded Edward, in the middle of the conversation, of the time, and they rushed home.

"Aw . . . Hope today I won't get any scolding," Rose said, fretful.

While driving, Edward consoled Rose. "Don't worry. I'll drop you on time. If they won't allow you to enter, then you can come down to my house, or I'll speak with him same as before."

"Thanks! But unfortunately I can't come along with you. I need to mark my entry. Otherwise, they'll call my real father," Rose exposed.

"If you're fine, then can I drive fast?" Edward said, seeking approval.

"Yes, I won't mind."

Edward drove the fastest he could and covered the distance of thirty minutes in just twenty minutes. This made it possible for Rose to enter without any trouble. Laura was waiting for Rose for dinner.

As things went on hastily, Rose didn't get time to inform Laura that she would not take dinner with her today.

Deviously, she entered the room, thinking, *What to excuse Laura for dinner?* She obviously asked, "Laura, please have dinner first, then I want to share something."

She went with Laura upstairs. Instead of pretending to be hungry, she confessed, "I've taken dinner outside." Laura was curious to know what was going on in her life and wanted to discern the reason behind the mysterious smile on her face since morning.

Laura got lost with the food, and Rose was waiting for her to finish. They came down to the room after taking dinner. Rose couldn't stop herself from sharing with Laura.

"You know what, Laura, yesterday night, I was talking to Edward, my manager."

"You're in love! He proposed to you, right?" Laura amazed Rose.

"My goodness! How did you come to know that?" Rose said, astonished.

"Well, I've been watching you since the last few days. Late at night, you're on the phone, and twice you went out. Now you're coming back in a car, so I just thought so," Laura elucidated.

"Yes . . . yes . . . You got the right one. I'm committed to him. Last night only he proposed me, and I said yes," Rose replied.

Laura was cheerful to hear Rose's love. They celebrated it and enjoyed as both had the love of their lives.

"We all four will party someday. Rose likes the idea." Laura shared the news with her boyfriend, and Jacob congratulated Rose.

He examined, "When are you going to introduce your love to us?"

"I'll try for the earliest," Rose responds.

Rose was blissful like never before. She had fallen in love for the first time. Indeed, she had liked him since she saw him for the first time at the interview. She was at the peak time of her career and love life, her both the life were running splendidly. She changed her clothes, lying quietly in bed, desperately waiting for the call, with lots to share with him.

Chapter 6

Rose hadn't received any call from the Edward since they got committed. She last chatted with him on the proposal night. Rose went to the office regularly, but she didn't get time to talk Edward as he was always busy with the monthly targets.

They had hardly seen each other after that dinner. This drove Rose concerned for her love relationship. She desired to spend ample time together, but unfortunately, Edward had to go to New Jersey. On September 20, in the afternoon, she received a call from Edward.

"How're you doing? Is everything all right?"

"Yes . . . I'm at the office. When will you come?"

"Dear, nowadays, my senior manager is on tour in New York, so I'm accompanying him," Edward simplified.

He kept the phone and got engaged with work. Hopelessly, Rose left early from the office and returned to the hostel with a dull face as she wasn't finding it cheerful in the absence of Edward. Rose attempted to divert her mind with the class assignments as she din't have any task to perform.

Laura acknowledged her. "Soon, your dream airline is going to conduct the hiring of a new air hostess."

"Wow! I'll start the preparation from now onwards," Rose said elatedly.

She was occupied with gathering information. Since she was good in English, she taught Laura regularly about the interview techniques and communication skills. Three days later, Rose met Edward in the office.

"I don't know how to say. Please don't get me wrong. My intention isn't to hurt you." Edward requested for forgiveness before he said anything to Rose.

"Please speak first," Rose cajoled.

"There's bad news for you, dear."

"What's that?"

"You must be aware that as per the rule of any organization, a couple can't work in the same company or the blood relations," Edward said, doomed.

"Yes! I know about the rule," Rose said in despair.

"Dear, people surrounding us came to know about our relation. If it'd reach the top-level management, then I've to quit the job," Edward informed vaguely. Rose was still unclear about the situation.

"Well, I can't understand you,"

"I'm sorry, dear. You need to quit the job. As a couple, we can't work in same company. I hope you understand," he abhorred.

This rule crushed Rose badly. She was deflated not because of losing her job, as she had worked there for three months, but because of Edward since now she'd rarely get the chance to meet him.

Edward sways her for quitting the job and comforted her for the other job. Forlornly, Rose agreed with his recommendation and resigned today itself. Since this was going to be the last day for her in the office with Edward, he took her out to optimism her with the treat.

Soon after the office time, they left for the lake-view side at New York. Rose was wretched about the job, but she was gratified with Edward and forgot the miserable news.

Soon after returning from the excursion, Rose immediately started hunting for a new job. She notified the incident to Laura. "I lost my job today."

"Aw . . . why? What's the reason?"

"Being in a relationship with Edward can't permit me to assist him. Otherwise, he'll get into trouble."

"Yeah, but why did you quit the job? He can also leave the company." Laura distrusted Edward.

Laura had qualms about Rose's love life. She was of opinion why he didn't put down the papers. Nevertheless, she didn't discuss this with Rose, perhaps to not make her feel adverse toward Edward.

It was time for Laura's graduation exam. She returned to her hometown, *Richville*, for a fortnight. In the absence of her chum, Rose worked hard hunting for a new job, and after a gap of one month, she succeeded in securing a job. Of late, she was working with a renowned educational institute as a career counselor.

Her salary remained the equivalent as before, but there was a slight difference in the working hours. The good thing about her new job was the nearness to her hostel. Subsequently, she could easily reach the office at a walking distance of fifteen minutes.

After her confirmation letter, she desired to share her achievements first with Edward then with her chum Laura; both congratulated her for the new job.

In a short tenure of a couple of weeks, she settled down with her new job but found it boring to return to the hostel after the office as Laura wasn't present. From the time her new job started, Rose didn't get the chance to meet Edward as her working time was till late evening, and Edward also left the office late at night.

The casual behavior of Edward and his lack of communication with Rose made her annoyed. She expected that at least if they can't meet regularly, then at least he can manage to give her a call.

A few weeks later, after office hours, she initiated to call Edward as they hadn't talked since the last week. Edward didn't pick the call but texted her, "I'm in a meeting now, will call you later."

It was tough for Rose to pass the nighttime without Laura and Edward. Nowadays, she didn't even go upstairs for dinner. Instead of this, she preferred to bring the food into the room.

As she was practicing this for a long time, once, she was caught and was penalized a hundred dollars. It wasn't enjoyable to go upstairs unaccompanied, so she brought the food regularly from outside. One day, in the evening, when Rose was returning from the office, Edward called her. "Where're you now?" Edward inquired.

"I'm leaving the office. On my way to the hostel,"

"Would you come out for dinner?"

"Yes, where do I need to go?"

"Do one thing: get ready. I'll pick you up from the hostel in a while."

Rose's happiness had no limits. She querulously strode to the room and dressed in the best seductive style she could. Muddled at what to wear casual or gowns, nonetheless she didn't want to waste time simply in indecision. She quickly put on her scarlet off-shoulder evening gown.

Edward took her to the newly opened restaurant in the countryside. After finishing their dinner, he brought Rose to show his flat where he shifted temporary.

It was a well-furnished single flat near Citi Financial office. Rose had variegated feelings as she was passionate for meeting him after a week's time. Contrary, she was worried as she hadn't visited any men at their personal accommodations before this.

No one surrounded the room; Edward stayed there unaided. It was a studio apartment. Awkwardly, Rose sat in the chair, and Edward sat opposite on a bed facing her.

He wanted to plan their future. "When are you ready for a marriage?"

"Anytime. Whenever you're ready," Rose gave her agreement.

"How many members are there in your family? What do they do?" Edward added.

"I've a nuclear family—my father, mother, and an elder sister. Mother is a teacher at Richville, Father is a retired accountant, and elder sister is pursuing her physiotherapy."

"What kind of groom are your parents looking for? Will they accept me?"

"Well, they won't have any objections with you. They just want a well-educated working man with a fair looking and should be in elite caste."

"Have you informed your parents about me?"

"No . . . I haven't disclosed to them yet about you."

"Yeah, please don't disclose our relation now. I will inform them later."

"Why not now? Aren't you planning to marry me?" Rose said consciously.

"Dear, you haven't got my point, I said that because you're too young now. You are running in your twenty-one and not yet graduated. I'd suggest you to first complete college and settle in your career, then we'd plan out for marriage," Edward said promisingly.

Rose felt quite disappointed with his commitment, and without discussing it further, she asked Edward to drop her at the hostel. Edward perceived her wrath. He came closer to Rose, held her hand, and delicately pushed her on the bed.

"I know you're angry with me. If I upset you, then I'm sorry, but don't leave me alone."

"Hmm . . ."

Gradually he brought Rose's hand closer to his lips and planted a kiss on her hand for the first time. Rose felt a bit cautious, but she didn't move from there though serenely relishing. Edward moved bit closer, sitting beside her without any gap. He situated his hand on her shoulder and touched her chin with his right hand to bring it upward, closer to his lips.

Gradually they drifted closer. Rose didn't know how to respond. She wanted to go; however, she loved the moment, but she was stagnant.

Edward drifted closer to her, kept his right hand around her waist, and pulled her against him. Rose slightly moved with her one hand on the bed. They were now facing each other; her eyes were down and half-closed.

Edward observed her eyes, touched her lips with his index finger, and slickly moved it over her face. This was such a wonderful feeling that Rose experienced for the first time. She felt a light tickling but didn't shuffle from that place, trying to be still.

It was just one-finger space left between these people. Abruptly, Edward's phone rang, and Rose dashingly opened her eyes and stood up.

The intimacy interrupted, Rose's mind got distracted whereas Edward cut the phone, but regrettably, Rose was ready to buzz off. Edward didn't want to stop now, but he felt a bit startled. If he forced her then, probably, she would break up.

He got ready, combing his hair and putting on the lights. Rose approached the door till Edward came. She tried to open the main entrance of the house but found it difficult to unlock the doors. While she was busy to unlock, her scarf stuck to the door.

Eventually, Edward arose behind her. Graciously, he removed the scarf and both paused for a while. The lights were off, and Rose's back leaned against Edward's as he was avidly behind her.

He sluggishly touched her hair and put them back aside, placing his left hand around her waist and the other hand on the back of her neck. He silently kissed her shoulders, slowly moved upward to her neck, and spun Rose facing each other.

He tenderly pushed Rose to the door and moved closer to her, uplifted her face chin with his finger, and kissed her forehead.

Deliberately, he came down to the eyes, nose, and at last, he finally grabbed her to smooch her. Rose's eyes were closed; both the hand round his shoulder enjoys her first smooch, lips locked for long.

Edward started stirring his hands above her waist, slightly closer to Rose's bust, and progressively, he tried to remove Rose's top. Edward wasn't ready to stop, and he started kissing her neck. He was surfing his index finger across her face, down to her neck, and his other hand was on her waist and tried to enter beneath her top, and his other hand tried to unlock her bra. Abruptly, he stopped when Rose pushed him.

"What happened? Do I've done wrong?"

"I'm not ready for that."

"But why? What's wrong with that?"

"Nothing. I'm not feeling peaceful. Please drop me at my room," Rose urged.

They left for the hostel after a cherished moment. Rose was silently visualizing the jiffy. She felt odd, confused between contentment and bashfulness. Edward quietly drove the car and wondered, *What's going to happen next? I wish Rose isn't angry with me. Hope she won't break the relation.* Edward craved while driving.

He parked the car ahead of the hostel gate and remained immobile. Rose surreptitiously picked her bag. After saying bye, she went out of the car.

Chapter 7

Earlier she came in the senses of the hostel manager. He noticed her entries and figured it out: since the last few days, Rose was habitually late. He notified it to the hostel owner.

Tonight, Rose had no chat with Edward. He also didn't call her. Rose was exultant but didn't understand what happened. She was standing at the window, surveilling the beauty of the night, vehemently wishing love to the blinking stars, and trying to find out the answer whether her act was right or wrong.

In the morning at 9:00 a.m. . . .

Knock knock. Someone was knocking at Rose's room.

"Who's there?" Rose inquired.

"Madam, please open the door. The manager is calling you down," the stranger replied.

Rose, distressed, opened the door,

"Yaa . . . Tell me what happened! Who's calling me?"

"Madam, downstairs, sir (hostel owner) has called you to his office."

"Okay! Tell him I'll come in ten minutes."

Rose thought for a moment then decided to get ready for the office first. After getting ready, she would meet the owner before leaving the hostel. She had no inkling what have been she called for. It was the first time in this hostel that this owner had called her; she had never met anyone before. She was petrified more than staggered, but assertively, she entered the reception.

"Are you Rose?" the owner inspected.

"Yes!"

"I've received a complaint against you that you're frequently late. I'd like to chat with your parents." the hotel owner clarified.

"Of course," she nodded.

Rose was stunned to hear this. She was unable to explain, and after thinking for a moment, she tried to skip meanwhile.

"At this time, no one is at home. Father has left for the office, and he'll be back in the evening, then you can call him."

"It's a critical matter. I'll be here, so you can come in the evening and connect with me," the owner ordered.

Rose left for the office. She tried to solve out to escape from this situation. Besides this, Laura wasn't in town. She called her to get her advice on the issue. Rose vomited the matter to Laura and asked her, "Please help me to get out of this situation?"

"Yeah, call your mother and excused her, because of the assignment nowadays, you're coming late. You can say her that you're with me, and we've joined the tutoring for our exams," Laura recommended.

"Thanks!"

Rose disconnected the phone and immediately called her mother. She explained Laura's suggestion and added, "If you don't trust me, then call Laura and cross-check with her."

Mother agreed with Rose, but she inquired, "Why do they want to talk to us? You can inform the same thing to them also."

"Actually, what happened was recently, we started the coaching classes, and we didn't expect that juts in few minutes late they'll mind. I was about to inform these people, but we weren't sure about our timings," Rose deceived.

Rose cunningly convinced her mother to some extent. She agreed with her daughter and was ready to say whatever she wanted her to speak when the owner was going to call them.

Rose exhaled and entered the office. Physically, she was present, but mentally, she was absent. Her mind was entwining last night's fantasies and thoughts.

At lunchtime, she received a text from Edward to call him when she gets free. Her complete day passed demanding in the career counseling of the engineering aspirants students.

In the evening, she reached the hostel and inquired for the owner, but he wasn't present there. She ascended to her room upstairs and gave a call to the Edward. He was engaged on the phone with another line, and indignantly, she disconnected the phone and started undressing. As Rose was unaided in the room nowadays, after being penalized, she had decided to reach the hostel on time before the deadline so that she could get dinner as well.

Unfortunately, again she was late by five minutes, and the canteen staff revoked dinner. She asked the staff, "Please give me dinner. I'm just five minutes late. Next time, I'll come on time." The staff repudiated. Pathetically, she returned without eating. The entire day she didn't get the time to eat, and in the evening, she rushed from the office to converse with her hostel owner. Because of this, she hadn't bought outdoor food. Famished, Rose descended to her room, wondering, *Aw . . . What to eat?*

The hostel gates were also padlocked, and she didn't know anyone else here except Laura, Jacob, and Edward. Out of these three, she already called Edward and opposing she never calls Jacob, remaining Laura she thought for a moment to call her but later dropped the idea assuming she was in her hometown what she'll do.

Her severe starvation made it difficult to sleep. She pondered to call Edward again, but she wasn't in a position to talk to anyone. Particularize every jiffy for the sunrise; subsequently she can go for the breakfast.

After hard starving lapsing night, 7:00 a.m., without sleep, Rose couldn't wait anymore to go upstairs and have breakfast. She even couldn't pass a moment to wait for the queue. She hastily grabbed the plate and self-served toast with a caper chino and sat in the corner isolated.

Without even concerned for anyone out there starts eating. She had never taken breakfast before in this hostel. On regular days, she left the hostel without any meals.

Today, while on her way to office, she detected a striking building was constructed opposite their hostel lane. She read the notice board and cognizant that a "hostel is going to be inaugurated by the end of month, admissions open."

Intolerantly, she marched to the office and called Laura.

"I've seen a superb recently-constructed building adjoining our hostel opposite lane. I investigated further, went inside, and saw that bookings are open for the registration," Rose pooled.

"When I return, we'll go and check its infrastructure and terms and conditions."

"Of course."

Rose wondered about shifting to new edifice following the last incident to call her parents. She started counting the days until Laura returned, and they would examine the place.

In hiatus of Laura, Edward and Rose had spent plenty of time with each other. They tramped at scenic lakes, Niagara hills, and the serene soothing beauties of the mountain. Once, at twilight, they walked to the park where Edward introduced Rose to his colleague and college mate and addressed her as his would-be wife.

Every single day brought Rose obsession for Edward. Her soul had established Edward to spend her complete life with him. She had a respectable place for him in her heart; however, she never divulged it in front of him but felt it.

Conversing at the beautiful place surrounded by a natural fountain, Edward bestowed all his contact numbers of his family and relatives to Rose including his entire family members. Rose, startled, asked, "Well, what's the purpose? What will I do with all the contact numbers? I don't need this."

She wasn't primed and intent to keep all those numbers, but Edward forced her to keep them all. She didn't fathom the logic behind it, but as a courtesy, she kept them. On the way to their house, Edward countered, "Don't you've any of your snaps?"

"Why?"

"I wanted to keep them in my purse, so that I can evoke you."

"I don't have any here. When I go home for exams, I'll bring them."

Whenever Edward interacted with Rose, she discovered an innovative thing about him, which brought her closer to him. She was desperately waiting for tomorrow as Laura would be coming after a fortnight. She woke up early in the morning, around 8:00 a.m., even though it was Sunday.

She planned to receive Laura at the airport. Regrettably, she was unable to crack it. She was about to leave and pick her up when, at the eleventh hour, Edward called her to meet. She accompanied him for some formal-clothing shopping.

They were scrutinizing for a deluxe brand at the busiest pedestrian junction: Times Square. Rose not only helped Edward in his shopping but she also chose all the dresses for him.

While she was occupied for the Edward shopping, he went to the soft-toys unit and bought a soft pink-colored teddy and rose-scented perfume for Rose. Edward gifted the teddy and perfume to Rose in private while they were in the car.

"Thanks for helping me with my shopping," Edward said gratefully.

"My pleasure. You're always welcome."

Edward drove the car with one hand, and he kept his left hand over Rose's hand.

"This's for you. Please open it now," Edward requested.

"Wow! What's this?" Rose yearned. "Oh . . . this teddy is so adorable, and the perfume fragrance is simply awesome," Rose praised.

"Thank God, you like it."

"Thank you so much for these divine gifts. Pink is my favorite color." Rose was electrified.

"Oh come on. Don't be so formal, love."

"You've got such wonderful taste," Rose praised.

"Yes! Since my childhood, I've been helping my mother and younger sister in their shopping so I gained a bit of awareness about it," Edward replied.

They finished the shopping before Laura's arrival time.

"Hey, it'd be nice if you could drop me at the airport," Rose entreated.

"Why? Are you going somewhere?"

"No, I'm not going anywhere. I told you before about my chum Laura. She is coming today from Richville, so I want to receive her," Rose expounded.

"Sure! No problem with that. We'll do one thing: You can pick her up. Meanwhile, I'll wait there for you folks."

"That's lovely, but she must be having luggage and her boyfriend Jacob must be there," Rose exposed.

"No problem. I'll drop the four of you. Please confirm with her that you're coming to receive her."

Rose called Jacob.

"Hi, what time is Laura coming?"

"She is about to come in ten to twenty minutes," Jacob confirmed.

"Fine. Do one thing: don't go anywhere. I'll be there just in a few minutes, and we'll go together," Rose ordered.

Rose rushed to the airport to astonish Jacob and Laura. She didn't bring Edward there, and he was waiting in the car park. Laura had just arrived, and thrilled, Rose reached her. When she observed her exiting from the airport luggage area, she sprinted toward her and warmly cuddled her.

"Hello, Jacob. Guys, follow me. I've a surprise for you," Rose greeted.

"Yeah, how did you manage to come here?" Laura questioned.

"Well, I wanted to introduce both of you to my beloved Edward. You guys haven't met him. He's waiting for us in the car park."

Rose fetched them to the parking and assisted Laura in transferring her baggage in the trunk. The three of them entered the car from three different gates.

"Laura, Jacob, he is Edward," Rose introduced.

"Hi, Edward, nice to meet you," Jacob welcomed.

"Edward, she is my pal Laura, and her boyfriend, Jacob." Rose introduced each of them.

"Hi, Jacob and Laura, nice to meet you sexy couple," Edward applauded.

"Same here," Jacob and Laura said in chorus.

Rose's contentment had no boundaries as she was accompanied by her chum and would be. Mingling each other for the first time. Laura displayed to Rose all the shopping she did for her from her hometown, Richville.

"Hey, how are these stilettos, scarf, and jacket I bought for you?"

"Thanks! All are sexy."

Rose also interchange with her about Edward while taking in dinner, homemade food which Laura brought. Rose explicates all the incidents. She wasn't happy with the amenities and the excellence of the services that her present hostel was offering.

"Oh dear, don't worry. We can go and find out some other accommodation," Laura solaced.

"I don't think there is a need to search. I've seen the newly constructed hostel, and I like it."

"Ah well, we need to go there and find out about the infrastructure and rent it," Laura countered.

"If possible for you, we'll go tomorrow after I return from the office," Rose probed.

"Uh–huh."

Chapter 8

At 7:00 p.m., Rose and Laura were dressing to see the new hostel construction. Rose was happier than Laura to visit this as she had issues with the current hostel management. Contrary, Laura wasn't ardent to change hostel again as she did it before—three months—and to an extent she was tranquil with the current hostel.

"Ah, the facade is quite attractive, isn't it?" Rose prodded.

"Eh, it is, but fulcrum this. We can't move here," Laura distressed.

Rose coaxed her best to agree Laura for shifting. At any price, she wasn't interested to continue in her current hostel because of the last few happenings. They entered the hostel and met with the authority. Astonishingly, it wasn't a male or staff member, but the owner herself was present here. She was Hillary. Her father had opened this hostel on her request.

"Well, where are you staying at present?" Hillary scanned.

"We live in the nearby accommodation," Rose retorted.

"Wonderful! Sundry girls from your area have recently registered here," Hillary educated.

"Oh, is that so? We don't know anything about it," Laura said, startled.

Hillary exhibited to them entire hostel area. "Well, folks, decide which room you want?"

She demonstrated to them the first story of which there was a left portion copiously reserved. It encompassed two beds in a single room. Unfortunately, all were booked. Contrasting to it, one big room was vacant, which was three sitters, and out of these, only two beds were available. While schmoozing with Hillary, they moved to the second floor. It had a variety of rooms—four, three, and two sitters were available. All the rooms had attached bathrooms. Hillary was about to take these folks upstairs when an office staff called her.

"Uh, could you see the rest of the floors and canteen by yourselves, and come down if you like it."

"Hmm . . . sure."

They ascended upstairs to the third floor. Above it was the canteen. This hostel was newly built, so all the furniture was in decent condition. Every corner was immaculate, and it was more commodious than the other hostels in the city.

The canteen was huge, and the seating capacity could occupy more than a hundred girls at a time. Laura was quite convinced with the hostel interiors; however, she wanted to ratify the food quality with the present residing girls out there so that they could get an accurate idea about the lifestyle.

"Hey, Rose, I think we need to cross-check with the current residents?" Laura anticipated.

"Uh, perfect. Gaze at that girl coming from the stairs," Rose indicated.

"Who?"

"Oh, look. The short rosy girl wearing indigo denim shorts, beige deep V-neckline top, holding a water bottle in her hand. Probably, she'll guide us better," Rose advocated.

"Excuse me, please." Laura stopped the girl.

"Yes . . ." the girl said.

"Well, could you please guide us about the food quality and the rest of the things in this hostel? Actually, we're planning to take admission here, so we want your help," Laura graciously asked in her soft voice.

"Ah well, look, here we get morning breakfast from six a.m. to nine a.m. daily. All day we've new cuisine. If we want lunch for college or the office then we can book that a day before. Lunchtime is afternoon twelve. Lastly, dinnertime is from seven to nine. The quality of the food is yummy," the girl acquainted.

"Thanks for such valuable information! It'd be a great favor to us if you elaborate further," Laura coveted.

"Ah, well, the cleaning is done on a regular basis, the security is good, the rent is affordable compared to other hostels in this area, the surrounding people and the owner herself are prominent—they themselves take good care—and the last entry is permitted up to ten o'clock," the girl added.

"Again, thanks a ton for your time," Laura esteemed.

Rose and Laura were excited after the information and positively scrutinized a place. They even forgot to ask the girl's name. After collecting the information, they descended to the ground floor toward the reception to see Hillary and discuss the rest of the details.

"So how's the place?" Hillary examined.

"Hmm . . . It's good. We want to shift by the end of this month. Please tell us about the deposit and rent?" Rose said, scouting.

"Well, the monthly rent of the rooms is five hundred dollars each, and we want one month advance as a security deposit that is refundable when you leave the hostel," Hillary elucidated.

"Ah, we're ready to take the first floor right-hand side room. Please book the two seats for us," Laura demanded.

"Okay then. See you at the end of this month, uh-huh," Hillary agreed.

The visit was productive and pleasing to both. They'd made up their minds for relocating. Laura left to visit Jacob's house, and Rose got occupied with Edward on the phone. She pooled her plan precedence to her would be.

Sluggishly, he admired the place. The next day, Rose and Laura decided to hang out together with their boyfriends.

They contacted their partners and asked them to come to the outing. Jacob and Edward luckily settled with their ideas. They went out to an adorable lake outside the city. Later, they planned to go on trekking near New York. Laura and Jacob walked in front, and Edward and Rose followed behind them.

Beautiful weather, mild sunlight, and a cold wind was blowing at its best. Edward halted at the side of the lake and stood against the fencing. He held Rose's hands, and the other one was around her back. He pulled her toward him, and they had romantic talks. Meanwhile, Laura and Jacob climbed upward, holding each other's hand. They continued with their talks.

At dusk, all gathered for dinner after the romantic chat. This was the second time Edward and Jacob mingled. Edward tried to explore Jacob's nurture.

"Basically, what you do? I mean what's your qualification?" Edward inquired.

"Uh, I've completed my engineering, and I'm looking out for a job."

"That's great to meet an engineer. What's your hometown?"

"California."

"What's your family background?" Edward continues.

"My father is a police in California, and Mother is a homemaker."

"Amazing! You come from an elite background," Edward praised.

"Hmm . . ."

The conversation went on. Rose and Laura were enjoying their dinner while their soul mates were busy in ken each other. Enough time these folks spend today.

Edward carried all in his car. First, they decided to drop Rose and Laura, and at last, Edward and Jacob left. In a short time, they mingled. Both chose to share a flat in Manhattan, near Edward's office, and it was also closer to their girlfriends' hostel.

The next day, in the evening, Rose and Laura acknowledged their boyfriends' matter. They were exultant for their partners as they also lived together. Days passed and these couples had spent a lot of time, and all of them were quite comfortable with one another.

Rose was at the office while she received an unexpected call from her mother.

"Hello, how are you, darling? How's your college going on?" Rose's mother asked.

"Hmm . . . All is fine mom," Rose said, worried.

"Good to hear this, darling. Your exam date came. It'll be starting by the end of this month. Make the reservation, and come soon at home," Mom asked.

"Well, I'll book the tickets in the evening and let you," Rose sighed.

Rose wondering for the home life. Instantly, she called Edward to inform him that her college exam date had come, "Do well in your exam. All the best," Edward wished.

"Thanks, but I need to go to Richville next week. I'm concerned about the tickets as I'm not sure with this short time whether I'll get the confirmed tickets for the flight or not." Rose said, distressed.

"Ah, don't worry about the tickets. I'll do it for you. You just take care about the packing," Edward promised.

She returned to the hostel and asked Laura to come out for shopping. Jacob also accompanied the girls like as always.

They left for their beloved destination, Times Square, where Jacob aided Rose to shop for her family. She missed her partner, but she didn't want to intrude on him during working hours.

It was for Rose family shopping but more than her Laura shop for herself, she also shopped for Jacob. Rose perceived the idea, and she bought a plain blue formal shirt for Edward.

At half past nine, Rose was relaxing in her bed, calling Edward. She had a lot to share with him. Unfortunately, Edward's phone was busy somewhere else. It was the first time Rose didn't mind, and she waited for a few minutes and got busy with her packing. After an hour, again she gave a call to him; the phone was still busy.

Rose ignored the second time, also wondering that he might be in the office. Laura was studying for her exams. Meanwhile, she discussed with Laura for their shifting to the new place. Laura suggested for her to postpone the idea until she returned from her home. Rose found it best to do the shifting later.

At eleven o'clock, Rose again dialed Edward's number, hoping this time they'd definitely connect. Hapless, his phone was continuously busy with someone else. Rose suspected the matter and wanted to investigate why he was so busy that he couldn't pick his phone up.

She wondered for a few seconds then got the instinct to cross-check with his roommate, Jacob.

"What is he doing?"

Rose approached Laura and consulted her.

"Hey, Laura, please inquire Jacob what Edward is doing. I'm trying his phone, it's continuously engaged," Rose requested.

"Uh-huh."

Knowing this, Laura instantly called Jacob.

"Hey, can you do me a favor? Rose is a little worried. She is constantly calling Edward, but he's not picking her call." Laura checked.

"Oh, let me check what he is doing," Jacob answered.

Slyly Jacob entered Edward's room, and after a few minutes' assessment, he informed Laura, "Edward is drunk. Right now, he's connected to a girl and is unconscious." Laura discussed the scenario with Rose and whatever Jacob informed her. Rose was no longer patient to wait any further, hoping to sort out the matter with Edward as soon as possible. Laura detected her vexation.

"Um . . . Darling, relax. Take it easy," Laura persuaded.

Rose was restless the entire night. She kept on trying Edward's number the complete night but didn't get a reply from him. This incident has turned Rose skeptical toward Edward. At the first instant, her mind wondered to break the relation, and on the other hand, she was occupied with the commitment. The gloomy, dark night drove her to drop him a message: "Edward, this is it. I won't call you for the entire life."

She was expecting a reply from his side, but she didn't receive anything. The murky, restless night was over for her; she felt dull and dejected in the morning, not in the mood to go to the office but tediously reached there.

With every second passing by, she was desperately waiting for a message or call from him despite the fact that she dropped him a relationship breakup message.

It was time for her classes. Today they had a final submission as well subsequent to the completion of grooming module of the aviation. Now onward, their grooming for airlines had started. At the end of the lecture, they'd been informed about the final dates of the Delta Air Lines interview at New York in the middle of next month.

Everyone in the class had started preparing for it. Laura also planned for the same and discussed with Rose what to wear for it.

Rose seemed to be the least interested in the preparation and didn't utter a single word about it. Laura cognized her and sympathized with her by suggesting to concentrate on her career. However, Laura's counseling wasn't working. Rose came to the hostel after classes and didn't turn up for the office.

At 9:00 p.m., Rose hadn't taken anything since morning.

"Hey, please take some food. He'll definitely call you. Please take dinner with me," Laura requested.

"I'm not feeling hungry. Please, you go and take dinner," Rose moaned.

"I'll also not go upstairs. You know it, daily we dine together. So how can I go alone today?" Laura countered.

Rose wasn't intent to take dinner, but for Laura's sake, she went upstairs and ate a little bit. Laura did her best to cheer her, but all her efforts were in vain.

At half past ten, Rose, was in bed, too tired after a long, hectic day as she didn't sleep last night so felt too sleepy today. Startlingly, she checked her phone for the time and saw the Edward unread message: "Please call me when you get free."

Rose woke up and moved to the window; without wasting a single moment, she dialed Edward's number.

"Hi, sorry for the yesterday. I didn't pick up the call, and the whole day I was busy," Edward elucidated.

"Where were you yesterday?" Rose interrogated heatedly.

"Uh, could you please tell me what happened? Was there something urgent yesterday?" Edward tried to skip the questions.

"Nothing much. I'll be leaving this week to my hometown. So I was asking you regarding the reservation."

"Oh well, don't worry about that. I had booked the tickets for you. Anything else, my love?"

Rose wanted to discern why Edward was busy last night on the phone, but she was unable to express anything. She dreaded every moment of losing him or making him annoyed. Neither did she express her anger or inquire anything else.

"When will we meet?" Rose probed.

"I'll let you know afterward. Definitely before you're moving," Edward replied.

Rose didn't want much from him. She was just looking for a little time. She had many questions but rests hushed. One day, before Rose went to the Richville, Edward called her to collect the ticket after office hours. Rose didn't go directly from the office, but she wanted to dress appealingly before she met Edward. She wore a beautiful halter neck top with denim shorts.

"Gorgeous!" Edward commented.

"Thanks . . ."

"These're your tickets for the American Airlines. All the best for your exams," Edward greeted.

"Thanks for your favor. Please take the money for the ticket," Rose offered.

"That's not needed. Keep this with you," Edward disallowed the money Rose offered.

Whenever Edward and Rose went out for a date, Rose paid half of the money for her side. This time also, Rose offered her ticket money to Edward, but he didn't accept. He was always annoyed of this practice of Rose and disputed with her many times, but she continued to practice it.

Rose finished her packing and shopping. She was waiting for Laura and Jacob to drop her at the airport. Jacob wished her all the very best for her exams, and Laura too. Rose happily left for her hometown. She had gone to her home after a long time. Making fantasies for the home-cooked food and to relax for at least fortnight. However, Edward's phone chat kept her perturbed. She was still intent to know the person on the other side, but on the other hand, she didn't want to be a skeptic.

At quarter past twelve, Rose landed at the airport, and her father came to receive her. She came from a middle-class family; her father came to receive their daughter in a rental taxi. Her mother had roasted all the possible varieties of food that their daughter liked.

All the people in the family still awoke late. Her elder sister also joined them. As soon as Rose arrived at home, Mother tightly hugged her and whispered, "Miss you, sweetheart. Love you so much, muaah muaah."

Rose got busy with the family. Her sister was also in the queue to cuddle her; this was the first time she returned home after she left for New York.

"How're you, idiot?" Rose's sister, Anglie, goaded.

"I'm good!"

"Look at her, Mom. She has become feeble," Anglie said, bothered.

"Yes! I can see that. She must not be getting the food of her choice," Mom established.

"Why do you look slim? Your complexion has also darkened," Mom asked.

"Ah, I need to go to classes and office by walking. We get food on time, but that wasn't up to the mark," Rose retorted.

"For a fortnight you'll be here. Just forget everything and concentrate on studies. I'll make you the same as before," Mom vowed.

"Yes, Mom . . ."

All the family members stayed awake until late at night. Rose had the dinner of her choice after a long time: chicken her mom cooked for her.

The next day onward, Rose started studying for her exams. The weather was at its best this is the winter going on, temperature down in minus. Anglie and Rose decided to go upstairs after noontime and study there until their mom arrived.

Anglie was too keen to know about her little sister's hostel life as she had never gone outside of her hometown, Richville.

"Life is too good outside. There are no restrictions from the parents' side. You're free to do anything," Rose revealed.

"Oh . . . is that so!" Anglie yelled.

"Yes! It is."

You must have visited the entire New York and nearby places," Anglie interrogated.

"Um, not all, but most of the well-known places."

"How many friends have you made yet?"

"Well, my best friend is Laura at present and some of the hostel mates and aviation batch."

"Who is she? Where does she live?"

"She's from Richville, of my age, and is there at my batch."

"That's fantastic! You've good company."

In the afternoon Rose's mother returned from the college where she taught.

"Have you taken breakfast?" Mom asked.

"No, no," Rose and Anglie replied.

"Come, take the lunch with me inside the home in open sunlight."

"So how much have you studied?" Mom asked.

"Come on, Mom. In the morning I've started," Rose exempted.

"Study well and eat on time. At least in this exam, score first grade," Mom ordered.

"Yeah, I'll try for it."

Rose enjoyed with her sister at noon. In the evening she made sure that she had a word with Edward. Since she came home, she didn't get the time to talk Edward, and he also didn't call her. It drove her attention.

*She thought to wait a day for his call,*but when he didn't call, she found the time and space to call him. She was uncomfortable to talk to him in front of family members. Her home was not huge where she could get a private and desolate space to talk. It had only three rooms excluding the kitchen. They lived on the first floor, and the ground floor was being rented. Rose and Anglie shared the single room. It was hard for her to find concealment in her home. As Mom came after two o'clock from the college, Anglie didn't go anywhere else but her college. That was also not regularly but only during exam time.

At ten o'clock, Rose discerned that her mom and sister were engaged in watching television. Secretively, she moved to her room and quickly made a call to Edward. Luck wasn't in her favor right now. She called twice, but the phone was busy with some other line.

It was late night. Rose knew very well that at this time he had returned from the office and finished dinner. A few minutes later, Anglie arrived in the room to sleep. Rose couldn't do anything but wait for his call.

She was lying in bed, against the wall, pretending that she was studying to Anglie. However, her elder sister knew her very well; she figured it out from her face.

"What happened? Why are you lost? What's going on in your mind?" Anglie grilled.

"Nothing. Can't you see I'm studying?" Rose yelled.

"Don't try to fool me. I know you very well. You're hiding something!" Anglie roared.

"Nothing like that. Why are you suspecting me?" Rose said.

"If there is something which makes you tense, share with me."

"Ah, there is nothing now. If there would be, definitely, I'll let you know."

Anglie was emotionally attached to Rose. She understood the unsaid feelings of her heart. She gave her best to make Rose spit out the truth, but all her efforts were in vain. Rose was a sturdy girl, and it wasn't easy to melt her soon.

Though Rose knew all the stuff of the personal life of her sister, Anglie, she didn't share anything with her.

Anglie's routine at night was on the phone, and she regularly chatted with her mate. The night passed by, but Edward didn't reply.

She tried to ignore it, but the idea of chatting with her partner kept disturbing her whole night. She planned to study at least one chapter tonight, but for the name's sake, the book was kept in her hand; however, her mind was negligent.

Early in the morning, her mom and father left for the office, and she waited for Anglie to leave the house or go somewhere else so that she could again connect with him in person.

At 12:00 p.m., Anglie wasn't at home. Rose, without wasting a single minute, closed all the doors of the house and kept dialing Edward's number.

At noontime, Edward usually was in the office, then also Rose kept on interrupting him. Initially, after one hour, Edward didn't respond. Rose's patience seemed to be over, and she threatened Edward by dropping a message: "This is it. I don't think our relationship will work further. After this I won't call you."

She assumed that, reading this, he would definitely call, but she was not right. At 3:00 p.m., her mom and Anglie returned from the office and college respectively, but she didn't receive a call. Forlornly, she decided never to call him and focus on studies.

Her mother wanted her to concentrate on this year's term and get good results. She had firmly decided not to call him. It was 9:00 p.m., the family was busy with television, and Anglie, at this time, usually got busy with her boyfriend on the phone.

Rose was about to go in her room and study. Abruptly, she saw her cell was vibrating; she marched there to pick it and was amazed to see the text from her partner. Mildly, Rose moved to the desolate place in the house and read it fully. "Sorry, I couldn't answer your call because I was busy with the work. I'll call you soon. Love you, sweetheart," Edward apologized.

Rose's decision never to turn to him ever in her life didn't last long as this text had reformed her mind and drew her back to him.

She didn't answer anything now but was eagerly waiting to hear his voice. Rose exhaled after the disheartening last two days. She restored her concentration over her studies, and her mind was stress-free.

Graduation first year exams were soon to be conducted. She deliberated hard for the results. In starting six papers, she hoped to score a distinction. Lot to go she had just two more exams left. Two more days were left; she had her last exams, and after that, she would move back to New York.

Tomorrow was Rose's last paper. She's cramming firm for it. She chose to finish the entire syllabus before 6:00 p.m. so that she could revise it in the evening. In the afternoon, at one, right now, Rose took a lunch break. She called Laura to know what's going on her end.

"Hello . . ."

"Hey, how are you doing? How was your exam?" Laura probed.

"I'm fine. Exams were good. Tomorrow is the last one."

"Aw . . . Good to hear this, and all the best for your last exams."

"Thanks."

"Come soon, darling! I'm waiting for you. Just come soon so that we can do the shifting. I've packed your entire luggage and mine also. You just need to come and shift there," Laura informed.

"Hmm . . . That's good. Let me complete it. After this, I'll be there after three to four days." "Okay . . . by the way, your partner is a gentleman. He's so kind."

"Why? How did you come to know about his kindness?"

"Oh, why are you surprised? You must be aware the day before yesterday, I met Edward as I was getting bored, so he gave me his laptop," Laura unveiled.

"Is that so?"

"Yes . . . you must be familiar?"

"Yaa . . . Yaa . . . Actually I forget that. Yes, he shared this with me."

Rose was amazed at this, unaware of their meeting. She pretended to know all in front of Laura, but in reality, she hadn't talked to Edward since she came home. Hearing this, Rose kept the phone and started weeping out.

Her soul was deplorable and couldn't accept it, but she didn't let anyone know. Anglie was present at home. All her plans for study were in vain as her complete day passed without studying a single chapter further.

The straining afternoon passed somehow; she controlled her tears. Late that evening, she couldn't resist anymore to call Edward. She kept on calling him, but as always, he didn't pick up the call.

A few minutes later, he dropped a message: "I'll call you later. Right now, busy with the meeting."

Night was over and Rose got ready for the exam; she hadn't studied anything after last afternoon. The exams started. She saw the exam paper, but out of six questions, she hardly knew three questions thoroughly.

Whatever Rose knew about the questions, she was even unable to write the studied questions.

Her mind was packed with her partner's feelings. In a short time, Rose had become affectionate to him.

Edward was her first love. She tried not to recollect him in the exam hall, but part of the time passed, and she hadn't even completed the two known answers. The exam instructor said, "Last one hour left. After this, no more extra time will be allotted."

Rose sped up to write, but the time was over, and she was only able to finish the four questions. Mom she returned home. All the exams were her finest, but the last one was the worst. She only hoped to just pass in this exam.

After a fortnight period, Rose was prepared to pack her bags. She had a wonderful time at home but was desperate to meet Edward. Her mother wasn't ready to give her permission for departure.

"Just one day over from your exams, and you're packing bags. Why don't you stay here for a week more?" Mom questioned.

"I'll come again after few months. At present, I don't have holidays. I also need to attend classes," Rose excused.

"Next time when you come, take more holidays from the office and college."

"Sure! I'll remember it and definitely try."

Rose didn't have any problem with the office or classes. She could certainly take off for additional days, but her authentic reason to go back was to meet Edward. She was overpossessive of Edward.

She wondered, if she gave space to him, probably, he'd move to someone else. All set for her departure, her mother reserved a ticket for a tube for her. She would depart at night from there.

At 9:00 a.m., Laura and Jacob were waiting for her arrival. She wondered in the tube if Edward would have come to receive her, but she only wished this as she knew, somehow, he would never be there.

Rose arrived at the station and got down from the tube when, unpredictably . . .

"Welcome back, darling! Missed you so much!" Laura cuddled and warmly welcomed her.

"Same here, sweetheart. I missed you too."

"How're you Rose? Does exams were good or not?" Jacob questioned.

"I'm fine, and the exams were okay."

Articulately, they moved to the hostel. All the things were packed in their room. Rose just couldn't relax anymore to meet Edward. Soon after reaching her room, she dropped a text to the Edward: "I arrived at the room. Want to meet you soon."

Today, they had not taken the hostel food but what Rose brought from her home. Rose wanted to discern more about Edward and Laura's meeting, but she hesitated to ask her as she had pretended to know all.

"Where is the laptop?" asked Rose, discerning from Laura.

"I've returned it to him the next day itself."

"Okay . . ."

"Which place did you people choose to meet?"

"It's the same. Our favorite destination—Time square."

"Nice place! It is . . ."

"Anything else you come to know about him? I mean, in general, you people must have some routine chat also."

"No, not much. We met only for a few minutes. He handed over the laptop to me, and straightforwardly, I came back," Laura responded.

Rose thought in mind, *That's better.*

"Hey, I've good news for us. You'll be glad to hear this," Laura said.

"What's that?"

"Do you remember last month our aviation tutor informed us about the Delta Air Lines interview at New York?"

"Well, yes, I remember!"

"Eh, their campus date was finalized at New York's best five-star hotels. Our half of the batch is going there. I'm also planning to appear. Jacob will accompany me."

"Oh, that is my dream airline," Rose shrieked.

"Yes, I know, dear! That's why I'm thinking we can also go there together. You can ask Edward if he can also come with you."

"Excellent idea. I'll ask him today."

For a moment, Rose forgot all and filled up with positivity, and her mind was occupied fully with flying dreams. Since childhood, she'd been dreaming of the flying career. It seemed like her dreams were on edge.

The next day, after returning from the office, she met Edward and didn't inquire anything about the past endeavors but was keen to go to New York with him to appear in an interview. They progressed to nearby places in Manhattan.

"I called you several times. Why didn't you pick the phone?" Rose yelled.

"I can't pick your phone all the time. I've several calls to answer in a day," Edward answered rudely.

"No problem then. I won't call you again in my whole life. Just drop me at my hostel!" Rose screamed.

"Oops, soon you get angry. I didn't want to say that. I was expecting you to understand my situation," Edward said courteously.

"Ah, I always try to understand you, but for that, you need to share something. At least once in a day you can take time to text me."

"Well, I'll try to do that. Now tell me how were your exams?"

"Good! I want to ask you ask you something."

"Of course."

"Mid of next month, Delta Air Lines is hiring for the cabin crew profiles across the USA. I also want to appear in that. All my batch mates are moving including Laura. I don't have anyone to accompany me. Will you come with me?" Rose requested.

"Yeah, right now I can't say anything, but I'll let you know by the start of next week," Edward assured.

"Thanks!"

After a short lucrative conversation, Edward dropped her at the hostel. Rose had just one thing running in her mind: anyhow she wants to be selected in the interview. She had started attending the classes seriously to learn additional about the company hiring process.

She was not only preparing herself for this interview but also training Laura in the English language. Nowadays, she was equipped with the submission of all the pending assignments, and Jacob was facilitating both. Soon after office hours, Rose allocated her spare time in acknowledging the company's information.

On October 1, 2007, Rose was voraciously counting the days to the interview date and Edward's acceptance to escort her. Needless to say, if he wouldn't move with her, she'd go along with Laura. Yet Rose hadn't informed her home about her schedule.

She probed her mother, "I've to appear in Delta Air Lines interview. It'd be great if Dad can accompany me."

Mom denied because of her father's unfit health for travelling.

However, she pleaded her father if he could accompany her. Unfortunately, due to his old age and the inadequate remunerated leave restraint of his government job, he also denied.

Instead of axing the idea, she started shopping for the airline attires and makeup. Imminent weekend Rose and Laura cherry-picks to finish the interview shopping.

Rose's prerequisite was to get a professional photo shot of her. Before applying for any job in the aviation sector, specifically for flying cabin crew, photos had to be in the aviation grooming etiquettes.

This varies from airline to airline. Rose congregated all the evidence about this company from the Net and from her aviation tutor.

This was the first time in her life that she had left no stone unturned. She was done with the photo shoot, as per the standards set by the Delta Air Lines. In a single snap, she wore a short navy skirt and a snug purple shirt tucked by a blue satin scarf and had tied a French bun.

The succeeding day, in the grooming lecture, Rose discerned that Delta Air Lines only recruited "flying models" with colored hair.

In the midst of lecture, and without waiting for a single moment, she instantly marched to the parlor for hairstyling and coloring. Passionate for the first time hair coloring.

Her natural hair color was mixed with brown and light black. She was oblivious with what to do with her coloring. After reviewing the shade catalogue, she finalized for light blond ten highlights.

Hair coloring had completely transformed Rose's persona. A new transformation reflected her like a professional model. Additionally, it had boosted her confidence level. Final preparations were done; she was prepared with the branded attire, professional snaps, and new look. Just the confirmation from Edward was left.

The moment Rose arrived in the hostel, eyes were keenly watching Rose for her makeover. Wherever she passed, she got a compliment. The heartwarming compliments elated her confidence.

At midnight, Rose was about to sleep when she got a text from Edward: "Meet me when you get time."

"Yeah, I can meet you tomorrow anytime."

"Okay! I'll pick you up in the afternoon."

Rose had no idea what transpired him suddenly. His call made her piqued, but she couldn't do anything except wait for tomorrow.

On a bright Sunday afternoon, Rose was ready to meet him. A dejected Edward was waiting outside the gate of the hostel. Rose sat in his car and probed, "What happened? You called me precipitously? Is everything fine with you?"

"Of course. Yes. I want to discuss about our relationship," Edward whispered while driving. Rose still didn't catch the matter. He took her to the immediate church.

"Why you stopped the car here?" Rose yelled.

"Eh, you will also go one day as you're aspiring for becoming a air hostess. If you get selected, then you will also leave me like Anglie," Edward countered.

"Ah, well, one day I've to go somewhere. I also need a job to survive, but that doesn't mean I'll leave you," Rose elucidated.

"Um, I don't know anything, but I don't want to lose you. That's why I brought you here at the church."

"What do you want to say? What's the purpose we're here?"

"I want to get married right now. We can inform the parents later," Edward dictated.

"What! What! Have you lost it, dear?" Rose yelled.

"No . . . I'm serious."

"This's impossible! I can't get married to you without the family's permission," Rose quantified.

"We can go to the priest and register. No one would know except us. Please, I want you."

"I respect your feelings, dear, but I need to take care of my family's reputation also. They must have planned something good for my marriage. Individually, I also don't want to get married slyly. I wish to invite all my relatives," Rose craved.

"Okay! If you'll get selected in the airlines, then you'll also leave me?"

"No . . . I'll never leave you. I'm always yours."

"Hmm . . . It's fine then. I'll go along with you to New York for your interview."

All the things had been finalized accurately for Rose. After a short argument, Rose was closer to him. But she wanted to detect more about Edward's past.

"Before me, who left you as you said?"

"Anglie! She was my first love. We've completed our graduation together. Used to live in the same flat in New Jersey. My family members had also accepted her."

"What happened then? Why did your folks brook up?"

"Yeah, after our engagement, I took the admission in engineering for her sake. There used to be my best friend who belonged to the same town I come from. He was also with me at my college. Anglie came in touch with him and left me and my family."

"Then what happened? Where is she now?"

"She is married and settled in New York."

"Oh, sad."

Day by day Rose explored in depth about his life. However, at present, she was engrossed to appear at and clear the interview process. As per their scheduled timetable, Edward had booked the tickets for all four. They left for New York on the same airline for which they were going to apply.

The four of them reached the venue straight from the airport to the lodge. Laura and Rose undressed in the airport changing room; Jacob and Edward waited for them and held their luggage.

The whiff of working in the airline delighted Rose. She hoped for the best for her selection. Laura, on the other hand, knew within about her rejections as she was poor in communication skills. They hired a private taxi, and fully groomed, they arrived at the venue. Rose reached the reception and inquired for their number.

She was amazed to look at the fully engaged waiting room. Rose said, "Laura, is there any chance for us? It's a long queue out there. All are nicely groomed and look smart."

"Let's hope for the best!" Laura solaced.

First, Laura had been called for the panel interview. "Good luck," Rose and Jacob greeted. Laura got ready, carrying her resume in a black folder and the required document.

Rose prayed for her and for Laura too. One by one, girls entered and came out after fifteen to twenty minutes. Suspense can be exposed only by Laura. Laura came from the interview room.

"How was your interview? What did they say? Were you selected?" Rose questioned.

"I don't know anything. They said, 'If you're selected, then we'll contact you soon,'" Laura answered.

"Okay! What did they test you on in the interview?"

"Well, they were general questions about ourselves: how we see ourselves after a few years, our views on the aviation industry, and last, about our qualifications."

"Oh, thanks for the information. Hope they'll ask me the same," Rose desired.

A few more ticks left for her dreams to emanate in factual. Just a distance away from the interview room from a waiting room. Finally, it was her turn. She had been called in; her partner, Laura, and Jacob greeted her.

All were desperately waiting for Rose to come out from the room and give them good news. The wait was over after half an hour; Rose exited drearily.

"What happened?" Edward queried.

"Move away from here. I don't want to continue," Rose said in despair.

"Is everything all right with you?" Laura asked.

"Yeah, what did they ask you?" Jacob scrutinized.

"Eh, I was selected for the interview. I answered all the questions right. They were about to release the offer letter, but at last, they observed my resume's last page. I forgot to sign there."

"Damn . . . this is such a silly mistake you did," Edward qualms.

"Let it be, Rose. Better luck next time," Laura consoled.

Maybe this was hard luck or a silly mistake Rose did, but she had a massive heart back to incident. She had been waiting for this opportunity for so many years to enter into this industry. Laura wasn't as dejected as she was prepared for the failure of her first attempt. Miserably, all returned from the venue and left for lunch as no one had taken anything since morning.

Rose wasn't interested in lunch; she remained quiet and aloof from chatting with anyone. In a rage, she called her mom. "Mom, I didn't get selected."

"First, you please don't cry. This isn't the last chance. You'll get many ahead," Mom comforted.

"I've tried hard for this."

"I told you, there'll be more chances in future."

"I know that, Mom, but this is the only one I wanted."

"Don't worry, honey. I'm there with you always."

"Thanks," Rose sighed.

Wishing for the next time, they left for New York the same day. Laura and Rose were rejected, but merely Rose was wretched about the rejection. In addition, Edward didn't have much distress in this regard as he wasn't much troubled for his lover's career.

All went back to their same routine.

Chapter 9

A few days later, Edward called Rose for a gathering and reminded her of the money that he paid on behalf of all the people.

In a nutshell, he was asking for Jacob's and Laura's payment, which he made. It wasn't much of an amount; however, it mattered a lot to him that was equal to a thousand dollars.

Rose quandaries as she couldn't ask it from her chum and couldn't disappoint her boyfriend also in such situation.

Without commenting anything, she returned home. Same like before, she had dinner with Laura, but that question still panicked her. She couldn't assemble the courage to ask her as it wouldn't look good; it might hurt her feelings as well.

Two weeks later.

Laura and Rose were engaged with their classes and jobs, sharing the same friendship as earlier. She was frantically waiting for some other opportunities in the aviation industry. During these days, her relations with Edward weren't as suave as before.

There was strain between Edward and Jacob since the past few days as they had been sharing a room for two months. Edward frequently drank at night. Subsequently, he didn't give time to Rose.

On the contrary, Jacob was always busy with Laura at daytime as well as at night on the phone.

The communication gap was perturbing for Rose as for her first love relation. She regularly investigated with Jacob through Laura. Regrettably, she was getting negative feedback about Edward.

When he didn't call her for a long time and didn't meet her, she averred with Jacob to reveal the truth. She acquainted that all night he's busy with someone else on the phone.

Rose's heart didn't allow her to trust this, but her mind knew this was the verity. Laura and Jacob didn't want to notify the truth as she was committed to Edward chastely.

Rose had started being cantankerous to Edward without revealing that she knew all the truth about him. Edward was a shrewd person; he also didn't disclose to her anything but had whiffed from where Rose came to discern.

As things were going erroneous, gloomily one more thing added: Edward and Jacob weren't allowed to bring their partners in their room at night. In spite of the caveat, Jacob brought Laura in on an afternoon in Edward's absence.

This incident smashed the lives of all the four friends. Instantly after the incident, Edward and Jacob no longer shared the room together. Jacob shifted with his other friends, and Edward shifted to his auntie's bungalow in New York.

They stopped interacting with each other. However, in the case of Rose and Laura, they were still at the newly shifted hostel, but bitterness in their relationship had developed.

They were sharing the same room but were dismayed because of their partners. They anticipated their partners to patch up, but thwarts from both the end there is no chance.

A fortnight later, Edward called Jacob, Laura, and Rose to his newly shifted place. All three had no inkling why they've been called.

Rose was frazzled for her both the relations, but blank for the Edward planning. The idea drove Rose exultant to see her partner, overlooking the past.

Edward had sent a driver with his car to pick her from the hostel. After a long period of a month, she was going to meet him; she clad up seductively to lure his attention.

Edward was sitting in the dining hall at his house. Jacob and Laura had arrived, and Rose arose a few minutes later. She had no indication about the matter, but she caught hot talks going on. She couldn't fathom the situation as she missed from the beginning but could figure out the fury in Edward and Jacob's conversation.

So much heat was in their discussion, which she could comprehend. Laura was mute at the moment. But when she aphorism Edward was dictating Jacob, she joined it. Before coming here, she was expecting to sort out between the two earlier buddies, but the situation is conflicting. In spite of that, both were fighting with each other on their previous disputes, but Rose wasn't clear what was going on but something regarding Edward's private life and about money.

The fight geared up; Edward and Jacob rose and started cussing. Laura interrupted in the midst, but Rose clogged both.

Laura grabbed Jacob away from home and fetched him to the out. Rose wanted to halt Laura and chat with her, but she didn't get the opportunity as she got busy with Edward, trying to appease him. Edward gravely maltreated Jacob for no reason. Rose couldn't express much except to cool him.

"Hmm . . . Edward, this isn't rational. You gratuitously called them and fought with them," Rose yelled.

"Yeah, who's more important for you—your friends or me?" Edward asked her in anger.

"Um, of course, you," Rose quandaries.

Edward's statement made Rose sentimental and passionate toward him. She couldn't favor Laura anymore but vulnerably supported him against her will. She recognized inside that Edward's brashness was wrong but couldn't go against him.

This incident had amalgamated with the earlier incident and together created gigantic a revolution in Rose's life. She may be near Edward, but she was scared to lose her best friend's other side.

After a long argument with Edward, his driver dropped her at the hostel. Her eyes were searching for Laura. Rose rushed to her room but didn't find Laura anywhere.

At quarter to three, Laura left long back from the Edward's place but hadn't arrived. Rose desired to connect with her. She picked up the phone and thought to dial her number but kept it back, memorizing today's incident.

Querulously, Rose passed every single tick. As it was Sunday, she was unaccompanied at the hostel. It's been a long time here for Rose in this city, but she never made any other friends other than her chum.

In fact, Laura never allowed herself to dialogue with anyone. All the girls in the hostel were relishing with their friends, and some were out, and the rest were grouped here in the cafeteria. Rose was starving but didn't have any company except Laura. Before this, she had never taken any company in the hostel.

In the evening at six, Rose was walking in the room, fervently waiting to dialogue with Laura. She hadn't yet taken food since last night, now in no more condition to bear it further. The entire afternoon, she had been inactive.

She simply sat unaided in the room. As for other roommates, Linda wasn't there.

She strolled out of the room. Straight to the last corner of her room, there was a small place to stand alongside the bathrooms for girls. She left the door partially open and surveilled the back view of her hostel.

Rose had no one except Edward and Laura in this city. Suddenly, an average stature, black hairs, dressed in pink-colored leggings, beige half-sleeved top emerged to use the bathroom. She noticed Rose was standing there alone.

"Hello, how're you doing? Long time to see you," the girl asked delicately.

"I'm fine. How are you?"

"I'm also fine. Just come in. Going for dinner. I think today they've prepared a feast," the girl informed.

"Ah! Delicious . . ."

"Would you like to join me for dinner?" the girl offered.

"Ah, well, thanks for the offer, but please, you go."

Rose was famished but couldn't express it as she had never taken dinner without Laura in this hostel.

She wondered whether Laura would take dinner with her or not. However, after working on the past, she politely refused to go with that girl.

At 9:30 p.m., Rose was still walking in the room, hoping that Laura would come definitely before the closing time of the hostel.

Yes, she was right. Laura arrived in the room. Rose desired to go closer and cuddle her, but she stayed stagnant and didn't utter a word. For a few minutes, she kept on observing Laura. She was busy on the phone, and Rose was counting the seconds for her to finish so that she could talk to her.

Laura leaned on her bed, and after the phone chat, she slept. Rose leisurely sedentary in bed and placed her hand on Laura's shoulder. "Laura, can we go for dinner?"

"No . . . You can go. I've taken my dinner," Laura replied foully.

Rose was dazed. She has waiting for her since afternoon for dinner, but she persisted calmly and said, "Laura, I'm sorry for Edward's behavior!"

"Eh, forget that. I need to sleep. We'll talk later," Laura answered coldly.

Rose wanted to sort out the differences between them, but Laura wasn't willing. Rose was in a bad temper, fraught with the spirits of losing a special relationship in her life. Night time for dinner was finished, and she hadn't yet taken single bite despite waiting too long for Laura.

She dearth loyal company for sharing all the glitches and for finishing the routine things with the person.

Adverse to pass the entire night on a bare stomach, she counted on the morning so that she could go to the office and order some snacks.

The next day at office . . .

"Ma'am, sir is calling you," the receptionist said.

"Okay! I'm going to meet him after five minutes."

"Sure ma'am."

"Please! May I get in, sir?" Rose said, seeking permission.

"Yes, please come," the boss permitted.

"Welcome Rose. You've done a good work for three months of your contracted job. We've cleared all your payments until now. Unfortunately, your contract is over with us, and at present, we don't have requirement for counselor. If the requirement arises in future then we'll definitely contact you. Once again, thanks for the services," the boss informed her penitently.

"Ah, that's all right, sir," Rose said in despair.

Depressed, Rose left immediately after the meeting at the office and dejectedly strode to the hostel. She tried to call Edward; as usual, he didn't pick up the call. She needed someone badly to stake the hitches of her life. She searched for Laura but couldn't find her in the room.

Without changing her clothes, she moved for lunch at the hostel cafeteria. It was a bit awkward to sit there alone and take lunch when all other girls were sitting there in clusters, but regrettably, she didn't have anyone.

Scrutinizing the scene, she marched back to the room without taking anything, but on the steps, she noticed the same girl approaching, carrying a water flask in her hand.

"Hi, Rose. How're you?" girls chortled.

"I'm doing well. How about you?" Rose countered.

"Hmm . . . Well, just came from college and starving, moving for lunch. Would you like to join me?"

"Yes, of course!" Rose quickly accepted the offer.

Both accompanied each other to lunch for the first time. Rose keenly desired for ages for someone to accompany her. Her new mate also took lunch most of the time unaccompanied.

"If you don't mind, can you please tell me your name once again?" Rose said gawkily.

"Yes, of course. I'm Payton Lewis," the girl retorted.

"Thanks. I'm Rose, you must be familiar," Rose familiarized.

"Yes . . . I know."

Right from the beginning day, Rose had been enraptured with Payton (the same girl whom Rose and Laura met when they came to see the hostel), but because of her friendship with Laura, she never got the chance to converse with her. She was gratified for a while to talk with her new pal. Her mind was trapped and didn't know what to do as she didn't have a job and her relations weren't with her. Once more, an extended, deserted day for her in the room; no one to talk with and nothing to do.

One week later . . .

Rose hadn't gone outside the hostel. She had no notion where to work and what to do with her career as well.

She wasn't attending classes any longer. Laura, nowadays, left the hostel in the morning and came at night before the closing of the hostel at 9:00 p.m.

Rose was sleeping in bed, keeping a hand above her head. She undergoes with the migraine pain. Laura was conscious of Rose's bug.

Whenever she had pain, she couldn't get up from the bed. Otherwise, she never went to sleep at this time.

Indignantly, Laura arrived in the room. In the first instance, she could easily perceive Rose was in pain. She switched on the lights, unpredictably sat beside Rose's head, and started clamping her head.

Rose was stunned. "Thanks."

"Yeah. No formalities with me."

This act of Laura had ignited some hopes in Rose's heart. She didn't say anything now—perhaps her pain didn't allow doing so—but relished this moment a lot.

Two days later, Rose met Edward; she conferred the complete matter with him about her job. She was hoping he could help her with regard to a job, but rather, he dampened Rose on her salary part.

She wanted a job that could give her at least a thousand dollars a month, but Edward underestimated her by saying, "You haven't graduated and have no additional qualifications, then how will you get a crack at a job with this amount?"

"Oh, I'll find it. Let's see," Rose roared.

She was expecting high with this meeting, but it turned up with no good happen. On the other side, she hadn't yakked with Laura since the last incident.

Barely, Rose returned to the hostel at night and was flabbergasted—Laura was packing her luggage. She was partially done; a few clothes were left.

Rose clutched around Laura and whispered, "Please don't leave me alone. I won't be able to live without you."

"Hmm . . . leave me. Nothing left. I've decide to shift."

Rose halted her from the relocating, but Laura didn't respond. Soon after, Laura was done with her packing. While she was sleeping, Rose turned closer to Laura's side and started coaxing, "Laura, please don't go. Please don't leave me. I'm sorry for all the endeavors. Why you're chastise me? We spent such a long time together. Please talk to me at least," Rose blubbered.

It barely shook Laura. She did not even trouble to turn her head to Rose's side. She was sleeping in bed with her back facing Rose.

Rose, after howling for an hour in front of Laura she didn't open her mouth for a once. She had cried for the first time in her life for anyone.

"Please! Laura, please don't go anywhere. I won't be able to live without you here. Forget all the things. I'm begging in front of you," Rose continued.

No reply from Laura's side. She was mum.

Rose was still in bed, sitting against the pillar. She had never sobbed like this before, weeping till late at night and not sleeping up to midnight.

At half past three, she had inevitably slept without taking dinner. Early in the morning, Laura and her roommate left for college before she woke up.

Rose noticed but still continued swaying in bed, but her eyes were open. She couldn't find the reason to wake up.

Previously, she had college and the office. When former reasons weren't there, she enjoyed with Laura, but now, she didn't find any reason perhaps to continue in this city.

At 8:30 a.m., someone knocked at Rose's room.

"Who's there?" Rose asked.

"It's me, Payton."

"Okay! Come in," Rose said, lying in bed.

"Hey, do you want to come for breakfast with me? It's going to close after ten minutes," Payton offered.

Rose quickly woke up and picked her toothpaste. "You go upstairs and reserve a place for me. I'm coming after brushing my teeth."

"Okay! No problem. I'm waiting."

Rose couldn't resist anymore for the food. She hadn't taken anything since last afternoon. In the usual days, Rose never came in the morning for breakfast as Laura used to bring it for her downstairs, but she was no longer performing any task for her. She wept badly last night; her eyes were sore and there was swelling under them.

Payton noticed her while she was taking breakfast with her and graciously asked, "Is everything all right with you? Your eyes are red."

"Yes! I'm perfectly fine." Rose didn't want to disclose anything to her about her personal life.

"So what's the plan for today?"

"Not much. I'll be here only," Rose replied as she also didn't know what she would do.

"Well, I've some work in college in the afternoon, then I'll come back."

"Okay! No problem. You can leave."

Payton left after having breakfast for her college, and Rose returned to the room. She flinched for the potential opportunities for the job but didn't know how to approach anyone. Last jobs she got were with the help of her associates.

However, she recently shifted in this hostel, and she didn't know anyone except Laura. Now she knew Payton also, but she was a student, and Rose hadn't shared anything with her.

The afternoon had also conceded but Rose didn't acquire whatsoever where to start with. After a squabble with Edward, she didn't want his assistance. She was frazzled with the existing circumstances.

She sensed to chat with her mother about the situation but dropped this idea, wondering, *Why bother her?* She couldn't share this thing with her family too as they were heedless about Edward.

If she would articulate that Laura was leaving her alone, then her mother would inquire the cause of it, which she couldn't disclose.

Deserted, Rose again went to sleep. As this time, she was alone in the hostel; all left for their routine mechanism. In this scorching weather, she felt the yearning for cold drinks. She evoked her home dreams when she used to eat fruit fusions and all the nourishing things during the straw-hat.

The dearth of money made her just fancy all those. If she had certain money then also she doesn't have anyone accompany.

At 3:30 p.m., Payton arrived at the hostel. She kept her bag in her room and went straight to see Rose in her room, expecting her to be there. "Yes." She assumed right.

"Hi, what did you do after I left you?" Payton probed.

"Nothing, I was sitting inanely."

"Okay!"

"You came too early?"

"Eh, because this is my summer holiday going on. We just requisite to go there for submission, that's it."

"Good, how was yours?"

"Well, I'm ranking second in the class this year."

"Cheers."

"Hey! I've brought a fruitcake for you, if you don't mind."

"Oh . . . that's so nice of you. I love it. In fact, I was wondering about it since this afternoon."

Discussion lasted till twilight in Rose's room. They swapped a bit about their existence. It appeared that both had a specific allure for each other. At 7:00 p.m., Rose desired to saunter out. She serenely asked Payton, "Hey, do you want to come for a saunter out? We'll have snacks in the countryside."

"Eh, sure, as you wish," Payton nodded.

Rose was accustomed to this place; she had visited it many times. She used to come with her friend Celestina, Laura, and Edward as well although Payton came here for the first time. Payton remunerated the bill as a civility. Rose attempted to overlook all the complications of her life and move forward. They came back sharp before the closing time of the hostel at 9:30 p.m.

Rose relaxed for a while in Payton's room. There was no one excluding her, but Rose made assured to move in her room before nine o'clock. She had been practicing this for a week.

She spent the day with Payton conversing in her room, and in the evening, they hung out, but before nine, she got back to her room. Payton detected it; for a week, she couldn't express it. Later, she gathered the courage to probe,

"Hey, what happened to you after nine at night? Why don't you stay in my room after this time?" Payton interrogated.

"Ah, actually, by this time Laura reaches the hostel . . ." Rose retorted. Payton didn't apprehend this as she was ignorant of Rose's life.

She didn't want to miff her by querying further questions. Rose practiced this regularly, expecting to retain Laura in her life.

When they were together, Laura didn't like Rose conversing with Payton. She wasn't having any problem with her, but she was possessive of her chum Rose. Despite the quarrels between them, Rose still maintained it for her sake.

It had been a month; Rose hadn't found a job, and she hadn't chatted with Laura and Edward. Laura was on notice period for leaving the hostel. This was the last month for Rose's aviation classes. Regular lectures were over, but her projects were due, which she hadn't completed yet. In fact, last month, she hardly attended a single class subsequent to her bangs and clashes with her chum.

A fortnight later . . .

At twelve in the afternoon, the climate was at its best. Rose was sitting with Payton in the hostel cafeteria, relishing on coffee and muffins. Not many people were there in the cafeteria, just groups of a few girls, excluding the canteen staff. Unexpectedly, Rose noticed Laura arriving in the cafeteria as she was sitting facing the door that could be visible from the entrance for anyone.

Laura perceived her obviously at the first instance itself but turned her eyes around. She grabbed a coffee and a packet of salted fries, went to the last corner, and sat, her back facing Rose. She was numb and didn't have a clue how to handle it.

She thought to go back or talk with her, but till Rose could take the judgment Laura left the cafeteria.

She dropped the last hope of retaining Laura. She knew it very well: Laura can't bear her with anyone. However, Rose had a soft corner for her; she felt immoral seeing her taking lunch unaccompanied.

All the folks in the hostel were aware of Rose and Laura's friendship. Individuals gave their example to others. This incident made all the people comprehend their breakup. Late at night, Rose and Laura had been invited to the birthday party celebration in the next room. Girls could easily ascertain the separate arrival of Rose and Laura.

Rose didn't want to attend, but if she wouldn't attend, then it would be weird. She was standing at the back side, and Laura was standing at the front. All girls on this level congregated noticed this.

Linda, their other roommate, had been witnessing their friendship since the first day, and now, she was the witness of their breakup too. She had been their well-wisher. As a best pal, she approached Rose.

"Nowadays, I'm watching you. Most of the time, you're with Payton. You and Laura are no longer talking to each other. Why?"

"Ah, I'm talking to her. She isn't," Rose said in desolation.

"Oops. I can only suggest. You folks look good together. If she isn't then, please, you communicate. The rest is your verdict," Linda condensed.

Rose slogged her best to sort things out with her, but nothing appeared to materialize. Both lived in the same room, their beds were also amalgamated, but it was going to be a month that they didn't turn up at each other. Rose anticipated every night, viewing at Laura to come back and waited for her daily to enter the room. Not a single day she turned.

The next day, Rose drove to her aviation classes to gather information about her assignments. She supposed there could be a company going to arrive here for the cabin-crew recruitments. She met her tutor and was ecstatic to accept that next week, American Airlines was coming to their premises. For a tick, she was agitated and wished to share it with everyone.

First she called Edward. "I've good news. Next week American Airlines is going to come to our center."

"Congrats! Work for that," Edward greeted aloofly.

The taciturn reaction of Edward distressed her from all the excitement, and later, she informed her mother.

"Wow! Such great news, darling. Work hard this time."

"Yes, Mom."

This wasn't over until she informed all in her networking. She was frantic to inform Laura as well. Providentially, she viewed Laura arriving to the center.

Without any hesitancy, same as formerly she said, "Hey, Laura, such good news for us. American Airlines is coming to recruit for cabin crew staff. Isn't it exciting?"

"Oh! That's great news. Anyways, I'm leaving now. I've an appointment with the tutor. See you later," Laura replied apathetically.

Rose couldn't stop herself from talking to Laura even after knowing her void fury toward her. Lastly, she returned to hostel and shared it with Payton as well.

"Hey, fantastic news. All the best," Payton greeted.

"Thanks!"

Rose was gratified to receive at least an encouraging reaction from her new pal. She had a lot more to do before the company arrived. Every airline requested diverse grooming styles. Rose pointed out the requirements from her aviation academy notice board.

She noted down all the requirements in her memoir. Scheduling to go out and shop all noted points with Laura as usual. Before this, they'd appeared in the all-inclusive interview together and went out for jobs search together. Excruciating delay for the Laura Company.

At nine that night, Laura returned as usual on time. Rose pondered a while that her bond with Laura may return the same as before after the small banter with Laura in the afternoon.

Before she could utter anything to her, she witnessed Laura was holding many shopping bags in her hand, and mischievously, she kept them in her cabinet.

Rose intensely scrutinized that she had bought new attire: a pair of black high-heel stilettos, a couple of scarves, and a bit of makeup.

It made Rose pledge never to talk any further as she was planning to go out for shopping for the identical stuff with Laura. It had disheartened Rose badly. Wretchedly, she decided to never retain Laura.

Merely two more days to go for the interview, Rose was excited but nervous and gloomy when she comprehended there was no one around her. She hadn't yet started shopping anything for it. She needed the same stuff that Laura purchased, but inappropriately, she didn't have ample funds. She pleaded with her mother, but they were willing to offer partly.

Rose was exasperated with the deficient funds and solitude at her crucial phase of career.

"Damn . . . I should cancel all," she whispered to herself.

Her heart still desired to appear in the interview though her mind daunted her.

At twilight, her mother called her. "We've deposited a thousand dollars in your account. Go and shop for your interview."

"Hurray! Thanks, Mom! Love you so much."

The influx of money had displayed a spark of faith for her juvenile nightmares. She was packed with ecstasy because of her clan's backing. She promptly called Payton. "Where're you? Come soon, please?"

"Oops, what happened? Are you all right?"

"Yeah, come first, and then I'll tell you," Rose said, creating suspicion.

Payton was busy at her college with some of her assignments. However, she instantaneously returned from the college on the entire way, vexed for Rose. She stormed into Rose's room. "Is everything all right?"

"Eh, you came immediately. Anyways, I want your assistance for shopping for my interview, and I guess you'll guide me perfectly," Rose retorted.

"Ah! You scared me. Anyways, I'd love to help you," Payton exhaled.

They left for Times Square. Rose loved terminus for shopping. This was the first time Rose

was going out with Payton. Instead of going in a private taxi, Payton took Rose on the local train. First, Rose wasn't ready to go as whenever she wanted to travel, she would call for a taxi. But to keep Payton, heart she travel in the tube.

Just in a few hours, Rose had completed shopping with Payton. Barely had she purchased a pair of stilettos, stockings, and makeup as recommended by Payton. Later, after concluding the shopping, she glimpsed at the store where she used to come with her ex-chum, Laura, to see if new stock arrived.

She entered the store, and the store manager identified her regular customer and said, "Ma'am, your friend Laura aren't accompanied?"

"No, she's not well," Rose whispered so that Payton didn't hear this.

Professional shopping was over, and they arrived before time. Rose's first journey on the tube wasn't as bad; she adored it. She suggested Rose economically.

Budget shopping which she do frequently. She was almost ready for the interview. Suddenly, when she reached the hostel, she evoked that she forgot to click the formal snaps for her interview.

Nothing could be done now. The hostel entrance was closed. Payton proposed to her to go in morning and take the urgent passport photos.

Interview day . . .

Rose dressed in a snug purple cotton shirt, ink–blue short skirt, a beautiful plain blue silk scarf, and aviation-style eye makeup. She got ready on time because of Payton. She facilitated her in all her grooming. While Rose was getting ready, she arranged all the required papers and documents in the beautiful professional folder then called a taxi for her to reach the academy on time.

Rose reached there on reporting time at 9:30 a.m. and confirmed her registration with the receptions.

Her eyes were searching to see what Laura was wearing. She sat in the queue. A decent crowd of around approximately two hundred cabin crew aspirants had come to attend.

Rose looked out at all the candidates, and after pondering, she restored her self-confidence. She felt honored for her attire after viewing the others.

Confident about her communication skills and the most imperative thing that vivifies her mind is the location and venue of the interview.

Rose's number was after a hundred candidates; therefore, she relaxed and chatted with other people around. Laura arrived late.

She was expecting a short talk with her, but Laura did not even bother to say hi to Rose. Rose also didn't bother her now.

One by one girl was getting less in number. Those who were qualified had been asked to wait for the next round; those remaining were requested to wait for their response later this month. Generally, it indicated their rejection. Rose's number was called. She was equipped to enter inside the cabin.

"Please, may I get in, sir?"

"Please be seated."

Rose answered almost all the six questions assuredly, and she got a positive response from the interviewer to wait outside for the next round.

She exited thankfully and enthused to share it to Payton immediately. First round interviews completed qualified candidates were waiting outside. They were hardly just fifteen in number. Rose's ex-chum, Laura, wasn't in the short list.

From their common classmate, Laura discerned the Rose selection. Envious, she did not even come to congratulate her. But things had changed; Rose has also stopped bothering about her. Out of all fifteen, the final six were selected for the final round that would be conducted after a fortnight. Gladly, Rose returned from the academy to her room. She notified her family and Edward and celebrated hard with Payton.

Chapter 10

On October 31, 2007, Laura was ready to leave the hostel. She packed all her luggage, and Jacob was waiting downstairs to transport her. It was her last day. Rose saw her from the hostel roof and came down and cuddled her tightly. Laura turned back and, after a long time, hugged her back. The last time they shared dinner together.

Friendly, she left the hostel, and Rose came down to see her off. Rose hadn't had any relationship like this before; this was her second relationship after Celestina in this city. Her reliance on relationships was a bit shattered. She gave her best to induce Laura but failed to do so.

Despite their jovial parting, when Rose returned to her room, she remembered her old days with her; it was almost a year they spent.

Rose had never spent such a long time with anyone before. When she was separated with Celestina, she didn't cry and did not even remember her, but with Laura, it was a long time, and she was involved with her ardently.

She tried to sleep there, but her gaze meandered to avoid Laura's bed, which they amalgamated when they arrived in this room.

She couldn't sleep secluded in this room but elected to stand up by the window in the dark room. At this time, she badly missed her true relations to be associated with her all the time.

She forlornly informed it to Edward as well, but he was too engaged with his professional career.

The next day, in the morning, she woke up early, took breakfast, and discussed with Payton for potential job opportunities.

They made a strategy to query their academy director if there was anything for her to work. It was horrendous for Rose to sit in the room unaccompanied all the time.

In the afternoon, she left with Payton for the institute and saw her director for the employment. Propitiously, he contracted to offer her the receptionist position in their academy.

It could make her at least endure in this city and stay on her own. She tactics to join later two three days after having some groundwork before coming here.

There was one more reason for Rose to stay in the city, and it was the challenge that she accepted from Edward: to prove to him that she could also get a job for a thousand dollars monthly, which Edward underestimated from her before.

In the evening, she called Edward and shared with him about the job. Edward wasn't engrossed to hear her much; just for civility, he applauded her.

Rose had a new challenge to face. Previously, she was having a breakup with some near and dear ones, but all of her relations have turned their backs on her.

In Rose's carrier, this was her fourth job, but in all her preceding jobs, she was enthusiastic to join and learn new things. She joined the office from today, but she was dull and had a lack of enthusiasm. It appeared that she had joined for the sake of monthly rent and for survival. This wasn't a new place for Rose to visit. She had been coming here since last year but as a student, and now, she was a receptionist here.

Dramatically, Rose's life had utterly transformed. Formerly, she used to hang out, wake up late, sleep late, giggle without any reason, and do a lot of witty things, bunk classes and do lots of shopping and many lively deeds.

However, now, she woke up early in the morning, took breakfast regularly with Payton, habitually went to the office, and after getting off from there, went straight back to the hostel, took dinner, and insipidly went off to bed after a one- or two-hour discussion with Payton.

She barely dialogued with anyone in the hostel except her roommate and Payton. All the girls in the hostel addressed her as haughty and sniffy. This may have been the reason because of her luscious guise like professional models. Indeed, she was the solitary girl in the hostel, which resembles like a model.

Her routine had drastically improved. She no longer went in her room. Later, after her office hours, she first went to Payton's room and merely went in her room to change her clothes or, early in the morning, to get prepared for the office. Rest all the time she rests in her new mate's room.

Rose had cleared the initial rounds of American Airlines interviews. The day after tomorrow, she had the concluding round. She hoped the best for this. She was virtually done with her preparation. Auspiciously, the final round was at her office. One of the senior managers of American Airlines was at New York today, in her office. Rose was clad with the same panache as earlier. Only six candidates for Rose to vie for the final round. She was the last candidate now to be interviewed.

"Please, may I get in, ma'am?" Rose said, seeking permission to enter the room.

"Yes, please have a seat," said the interviewer.

"Thanks! Good morning, gentlemen," Rose greeted.

"Well, you've got all the obligatory potential for the cabin crew profile. I'm pleased to meet a candidate like you," the interviewer admired.

"I appreciate your kindness, sir," Rose replied.

"Tell me whether you're ready to relocate anywhere in America?" the interviewer questioned.

"Yes, anywhere as per the company requirement."

"Great! Okay, tell me one last thing: What do you expect from the company? What is your salary expectation?"

"Anything that best suits my profile. I expect the best from American Airlines."

"Excellent! Can you please come and finally measure your weight for us?"

"Sure."

Till the time Rose stood and measured her weight for the interview's sake, he had already taken out the offer letter and pen. He, in fact, signed the copy and was ready to offer it to her. Suddenly, he stopped.

"I'm extremely sorry for this, but you cannot get the confirmation now. You just lack one kg in weight. You're forty-nine kg. As per company policy, we need fifty kg. I apologize, You're perfect, but gain some more weight, and surely, come next time," the interviewer abhorred.

"Ah, absolutely, sir."

Smashed, Rose left the room and got back to her work. She was extremely thwarted with today's interview. After clearing the five rounds, she was rejected just for one kilogram of weight. Rejection had made her to promise never to appear in the aviation industry in the future. She had been trying hard in her life to get into this industry, but things weren't working right.

She didn't want to share the disqualification with her family nor with Edward. However, she informed Payton.

Two weeks later, Rose was strolling in the evening time with Payton; there, she met Edward for a few notes in the ice cream parlor. Edward knew about her parting with Laura, but he was happy for it and acrimonious toward her. They stood outside the parlor, and Payton waited for them on the roadside.

Edward inquired Rose about the amount that she owed to Laura. He starkly said, "Have you thrown the money in her face?"

"Yes, I did," Rose answered giddily.

Payton didn't get embroiled in their banter as she was still oblivious to Rose's love life and her past relationships with Laura, but she loathed her attitude toward Laura. The way Rose was jesting about her ex-chum made her surprised about Edward's nature.

She wasn't cunning but had a sense of men's psychology, which made Edward's first impression worse. After a short meeting, Edward dropped them at the hostel in his car. Edward calumny Rose for Laura though she wasn't used to be like this. She had adored her true relationship, but his company made her think deleterious about her. She had no more regrets of their breakup.

In spite of the fact that Rose never wanted to work in the education sector and she may not be happy about her current job, she was in the right place.

This place offered her the platform to enter her dream industry. One more opportunity for her, hotfoot Delta Air Lines was going to conduct one more career opportunity with their company at the same city as before, but venue is different.

This was the second time in this last quarter of the year. However, Rose wasn't agitated this time but happy to acknowledge this.

She never coveted to omit this opportunity, but she lacked backing. Presently, she didn't have any interaction with her batch mates, and there was no one in the hostel of her batch. She couldn't ask Father as she was aware that her father couldn't travel much.

She was not working this time for the interview after last time's rejections. Additionally, because of seclusion. Further, to appear, she didn't have the adequate funds to pay for back and forth. In the evening time, she got back to the room and spoke to Payton regarding it. Payton got enthusiastic to hear this.

"Wow! This is such good news. So have you planned for it or not?"

"No, I can't go there alone. Let's see some other time."

"Hey, why not this time? You shouldn't miss it. Maybe your life may change after it."

"I'm aware of it but can't find the reliable company."

"Hey! Why don't you ask your partner, Edward?"

"Ah, he won't be able to go. He is bloody busy at his work."

"At least you can try once. He may get swayed and turn up. Huh."

"Eh."

The light of hope was enlightened once again for Rose. Payton left the room so that Rose could chat with her partner. She swiftly asked her, "What did he say?"

"Edward didn't say yes, but neither did he deny as well. He'll inform me after a couple of days."

Two days after . . .

Rose's mobile quivered.

"Unread text"

She quickly opened it: "I've booked the ticket, and we'll leave at night for New York and come back on Monday evening," Edward texted.

Rose was elated to get one more chance to spend time with Edward aside from attending the interview.

She was fretful more about her love relationship than her career at this stage. Rose didn't inform her family; rather, she took Payton's help to seek leave for two days from the hostel.

She mentioned in the register that she was going out with family, and Payton will look after it.

On June 16, 2008, with Payton's aid, Rose left with Edward at night at ten o'clock. He came with his driver to pick her up. Rose eyes bliss in anything rather to watch Edward.

She perceived all about him. Gently she sat in the car, but her mind was solicitous to Edward. Every time she met him, she felt like she was meeting him for the first time.

At 12:00 a.m., Rose's cell rang.

"Payton is calling."

"Many happy returns of the day," Payton greeted.

"Thank you so much. How did you come to know about this?"

"Well, I saw your admission form. Anyways, all the very best."

This was Rose's first birthday that she was with the love of her life. Edward also greeted her at twelve sharp. To devote stint with him she switched off her cell. Nocturnal elapsed and they didn't kip the entire night.

This time, they stayed at Edward's father's guesthouse. Rose's interview was over early morning itself, results are waiting. Edward was bushed after a chaotic day; they didn't wander anywhere. Instead, he reposed in the guesthouse.

They've been allotted a single room where Edward dozed, and Rose passed the time simply standing up by the window.

At twilight, they got ready to depart for New York. Edward booked the two tickets; one wasn't confirmed. The entire night, they travelled in the economy class where Edward lay down on Rose's lap. She couldn't say no to Edward and stayed awake to comfort him.

This journey had made Rose more affectionate with him. Payton was ready to welcome Rose with the surprise gift that she made in her absence: a stunning handmade birthday card.

Rose adored cards considerably, but no one presented her with such a gift before.

It was time to go for second semester exams at the end of this month. She had already applied for the leave application in the office. Her mother had booked the tickets for her at least a week before the exams.

On November 25, 2008, Rose was distressed to hear from Edward that he got promoted one level up in his career, and now, he'd be handling all the New York branches of Citi Financial, handling them through the main branch at New Jersey. He'd occasionally come to Manhattan. She was happy for his career growth although wretched about his new location. Edward asked Rose to meet him in New Jersey before she left for her exams.

It was quite difficult to accomplish it for him as Rose's mother had already reserved the tickets for her, and she wanted Rose to come along with her father while he returned from New York on the same day at home.

On the other hand, she had never visited New Jersey, and she didn't have anyone out there. Rose never wanted to miss any chance to meet him, especially not at this moment, and she hardly got a chance to meet him twice in a month.

She was timid about the distance as well. Somehow, Rose managed to convince her mother and postpone the tickets for four days.

She lied at her home that she isn't getting off from her office to come early at home. It was not over yet; she had to find out how she'd travel to New Jersey.

This was the month end, and Rose didn't receive her salary. She was left with a thousand bucks. Nowadays, whenever a problem arose, Rose took Payton's counsel, and she got the perfect solution for it.

Payton dropped her at the airport and made the arrangements for her tickets as well. She handled the hostel authorities by lying for Rose that she had gone out for an official tour.

Rose was once again travelling with economy class service just because of dearth of money. Edward already out at New Jersey with his car to receive her.

At half past nine, Rose arrived in New Jersey, and after freshening up, Edward took her to a movie. Rose relished the last show with him.

She was a bit petrified and edgy as she was staying at Edward's uncle's house. Earlier, many times, she met with him but never stayed with him at nighttime.

They returned from the movie, and as all the rooms were employed in the house, Edward brought Rose to his room. First, she rebuffed, but later, she agreed. Rose used his bathroom to change clothes. Two at night slight winter has started no one at home and pin drop silence.

Rose emanated from the washroom and used the dressing table to comb before she went to bed. Edward was frantically waiting for her to come; he watched Rose profoundly and went closer to her, pushed her to bed, and kissed her hand and forehead, and progressively, he brought his lip closer to her. Suddenly, then Rose paused him.

"Edward, I'm not comfortable."

"Why, but what's wrong?" Edward asked gently.

"I'm not prepared for this. I can't cross my limits."

"Don't you love me? We'll get married in the future. There is nothing wrong in it," Edward coaxed her.

"I've never been in any relation before. I'm not prepared for it."

"Yeah, tell me, if I'll not come to you then where will I go?" Edward continued.

They slept today in the same bed without any intimacy or lovemaking. Edward got a little thwarted by this.

The next day, he left for the office at 9:00 a.m., and Rose spent the entire day in his house, waiting for him. The entire day, she kept on wondering about her relationship, and at last, she didn't want to lose or disappoint her partner on any condition.

One late evening, Edward returned from the office and went to see the last movie show as this was a weekend.

One night, Edward was effusively electric and vanquishes Rose for sex. She hasn't idea fully heedless of it. Edward tried it once and didn't succeed today as Rose was a virgin. She couldn't bear the pain and ended up screaming.

Amidst they left it and opted to sleep. Edward's efforts succeeded on Sunday night when Rose lost her virginity. She was content to please her partner but startled a lot for her deed. She was troubled for her vulnerable sex last night, worried if she'd get pregnant, but Edward consoled her, "Don't worry, you won't get pregnant. I did sex during safe period and didn't insert it deep."

On Monday morning, she left for New York, from where she'd be travelling to her hometown, Richville. In the evening, she came to the hostel. Payton was glad to receive her and see her off in the morning again.

Rose shared her weekend with her but didn't disclose about her night life. When Payton asked her, "Where did you stay at night?"

Rose answered, "I was in a separate room."

Chapter 11

Rose felt mortified to share the New Jersey weekend's incident with anyone. After an overnight discussion, in the morning, Payton escorted her to the airport.

Rose hadn't crammed anything in this semester, yet there were just three days left for her first exam. All the course material was ready at her home as her mother bought it before she arrived.

Her parents scolded her for not coming home before a week's time as vowed by her during last semester. She shunned the conversation with them and wished to bond somehow with Edward.

The moment she reached home, she started calling Edward, but he didn't respond to her call anymore. Rose wanted him to introduce at home and get engaged. Because Edward wasn't responding to the phone, Rose dropped him a text for their engagement.

She didn't get any call from him; nevertheless, she received a text: "Don't irritate me by calling constantly."

This text had completely shaken her senses. Just two days left for her exams and Rose was lost with Edward's eerie behavior.

After getting physically involved with Edward, Rose wanted to turn this relationship into marriage. She already came home late by allotting him time, which she kept for her studies, and now, she was stunned by his insolent behavior.

Consistently, Rose's mind marveled for her love life, and she spoiled her exams. Half of the exams were finished in which Rose had spent time just waiting for his text. She wrote nothing in these exams.

She tried to focus on her remaining exams but couldn't. In this fortnight, she had given a myriad of calls to Edward, and not a single time was she called back. Instead, she got an offensive text, which she never anticipated from her love.

Anglie could notice the strain on Rose's face. Her nature was completely transformed; she was no more like earlier, when they used to chitchat and laugh without any reason, and Rose used to talk with her a lot.

Rose no longer dialogued with her family, but all day, she was lost in her own world. Anglie figured it out and forcibly asked her to share with her the cause for her strain.

At midnight time, Rose disclosed about Edward to Anglie, but she didn't reveal their physical relationship, which was the main reason for her strain.

Anglie, in the first instance, was delighted to know that Rose loved someone who belonged to the elite family and was additionally highly educated and handsome. But she had qualms on Rose and asked, "Have you crossed the limits?"

"Eh, there is nothing like what you're thinking," Rose fibbed.

Contrary to Rose's statement, Anglie suspected Edward's behavior. She wasn't persuaded by Rose's arguments.

She framed the worthy chunk about Edward and didn't disclose anything wrong about him. Anglie proposed to her to discover further about Edward.

"How will I come to know about him?" Rose countered startlingly.

"You forget my boyfriend is an astrologer too. He is good palmist as well," Anglie responded.

Rose recalled that her sister was committed to a son of their chaplain. Anglie loved him since she has been in eight classes. No one was conscious of it except Rose in her home. Her partner was blessed with some of supernatural powers. Anglie connected with him on the phone and handed over the cell to Rose. She expounded her situation and appealed for the recommendation.

Anglie's boyfriend queried for Edward's photograph. Furtively, Rose had taken Edward's snaps. She displayed that snap to him. Bluntly, he advocated to Rose, "Never trust this guy. He'll not marry you."

Anglie trusted her partner a lot and warned Rose to stay away from him. Rose's mind relied on his words and wanted to follow them, but her heart dictated the situation. Predication had devastated Rose's trust in her love relationship. It was Rose's second of college which was wicked until date. Not a single exam of Rose was good. She was sure to reset some of her exams.

She stayed merely for a week after the exams and returned to New York for her job. Inspecting Edward's behavior, she made up her mind not to meet him.

However, the day she reached New York, she received a text from him: "Meet me as soon as possible."

Rose eluded it for a couple of days and didn't reply and continued with her job. It didn't last long; Edward called her the next day at noontime. Rose was in the office.

"What happened, darling? Why are you not replying to my messages?" Edward asked.

"I'm in the office. You also didn't respond to my calls when I was at home." Rose cleverly answered.

"I'm apologetic for that. I was busy with work. Let's forget all and meet up on Sunday, and I'll pick you from the hostel," Edward expounded.

"Okay!" Rose countered.

To shun Edward was challenging for her. She couldn't say no to him. On Sunday afternoon, Edward picked Rose and brought her to his room.

He did his best to convince Rose again and fascinate toward him. He tranquillizes well about their marriage and made Rose down in front of him. Edward once again succeeded in his way to make a physical relationship with her. She forgot her sister's warning and the prediction of her would-be brother-in-law.

Moreover, moved by him after their meeting, Rose was once again positive about Edward. She restored the hopes for their marriage and cheerfully returned to the hostel.

One week later . . .

Rose received a confirmation e-mail about being short-listed for the Delta Air Lines for which she appeared in the interview at New York with Edward. Her family was overwhelmed at the news, and she was too, but when she informed it to Edward, he didn't react opportunely to this.

Rose has been waiting for a long time to fly. This final round could be the route for her to fly. At the end of the month, she'd be appearing in the final round as per the scheduled date given to her. She got ready with all the preparations and desired Edward's favor once again to join her, but he denied this time and screamed gravely at her.

He wasn't in approval of the Rose's flying career. He didn't indicate it openly, but passively, he wasn't ready to accompany her.

Just a week to go, and she may be flying. At the eleventh hour, Edward wanted to meet her at his house.

Rose went to see him at his house in the evening, expecting to spend quality time with him before leaving for the interview. Edward was in a different mood today; he sobbed badly in front of her and appealed, "You'll also leave me?"

"Why would I leave you?"

"If you'll get selected in the interview, then you'll go to a different country and will definitely forget me," Edward said, crying.

"No! I'll never leave you. I love you so much, Edward," Rose stated.

"Promise me you'll never leave me," Edward, holding Rose's hand, demanded.

Rose couldn't stop her emotions for him and gave him a vow. Edward once again committed her for marriage when she'd complete her graduation.

Rose agreed with his promise and had rather dropped the idea to even fly anymore. To please him, she didn't appear in the final round and was no longer interested to apply for any airline in future. She didn't hate this industry but only relinquished it for the sake of her love.

Rose continued with her job of front office executive. It was not adequate for her to survive, but she managed to do so, waiting for her graduation and, subsequently, marrying him.

She wasn't well, suffering from a severe flu, and had taken a week off, resting in the hostel deprived of medications.

In the afternoon, Edward called her not to inquire about her health but her favor to recruit a female assistant under him for the New York location. He had finally shifted to New Jersey and fortnightly visited New York.

Rose sent him the number of her colleague who was working with her at the same office. He didn't inquire anything related to her health and put down the phone.

It had been a month since Rose met him last time. She wanted to interact with him or at least talk to him daily, but Edward sidestepped this by giving excuses that he was busy with his family. After a week, Rose joined the office. Her colleague came to see her.

"Thanks, Rose"

"Hmm . . . For what?" Rose asked, surprised.

"Because of you, I got the job with such a good brand."

"How? I mean, please elaborate," Rose requested.

"You must be cognizant that Edward offered me a handsome package and good profile."

"Yeah, I know. Congratulations! By the way, when did you get this offer?" Rose pretended.

"Sunday evening, he called me at Costa coffee shop. There, he finalized."

Rose was traumatized to hear this. She pretended in front of her that she knew everything, but in reality, she was oblivious.

The moment Edward got the number from Rose, he gave a call to that number and scheduled a meeting in the evening at the Costa coffee shop. There, he finalized with her on the spot.

Rose couldn't bear this. She was ailing that day and had been demanding Edward to meet her once for a month, but he exempted saying that he was with his family.

He deceived her. Rose had caught Edward this time and dropped him a punitive message that their relationship was over.

Edward noticed it and immediately kept on calling Rose, but she didn't pick a single call from him. Later on, Edward called her friend Payton to talk about the Rose matter. She wasn't in town when the incident happened. Edward requested her not to reveal that he had called her.

Payton reached the hostel in the evening. She entered Rose's room and could watch her standing by the window in the dark, lights off, and she was sobbing badly.

"What happened? Is everything all right?" Payton inquired.

"Nothing, I just want space. Leave me alone."

"I can't leave you in this situation. Please tell me," Payton insisted.

"You won't understand. I'll be all right."

Payton didn't leave her and cuddle her from the back tightly, and she whispered, "Rose, I'm with you, darling. Please explain."

Rose quilted and spit the complete scene. Payton couldn't understand, but she was pretty sure about Edward's conduct. Since the first day itself, she suspected him but couldn't say directly to her.

Payton was in a dubious situation whether to share Edward's call with her or not. However, to reveal the truth was more important for her than keeping Edward's enigmas. Rose was wounded with her relationship, and when Payton disclosed Edward's call, she went into trauma again.

She esteemed Payton's loyalty to her. Their relationship had taken a new turn; Rose had sundry things concealed in her heart about Edward that she couldn't share to anyone though she conferred to Payton.

Rose said, "He is so desperate to make networking to new girls. He's a yearning male. He's psycho about girls."

"What are you saying?" Payton yelled.

"Yes! Earlier also he had contacted a lot of my friends, and I've seen he had many girlfriends in his mailing list and also in his contact list. Not only this, his cell phone is engaged all the time at night," Rose divulged.

"OMG! Thank God I didn't entertain him. Really, I can't visualize meeting him," Payton replied in a shocking mood.

Rose had been suspecting him soon after the first month of their relationship, but she never got any clue against him. Payton also counseled her same as sister told her to stay away from him and try to forget him. Rose resolutely decided it earlier but couldn't uphold. She already compromised a lot because of her love life, but now, she decided to focus on her dream to fly again.

She underway applying for the jobs on a regular basis and checked the interview dates. One of her batch mates, and presently her colleague, Maria had joined the front office with her. She was also searching out for aviation jobs.

Rose came to know from Maria that she's going to appear next week at the Qatar Airways interview in Dubai. This could be an international platform for anyone.

Rose and Maria both didn't have ample funds to spend but coped to arrange the travelling expenses and also accommodations.

Rose didn't want to miss this opportunity and joined her friend Maria. They decided to stay at the cheapest hotel in Dubai and came back same day.

It was going to be the biggest platform Rose could ever get.

They left for the interview with the cheapest airline tickets. One of their old batch mates was also going to join them who also Maria's girlfriend.

Rose was fairly affirmative about her selection as she knew her skills well, and her looks were also perfect for this international criteria for flying.

First, Maria has been called for an interview, then Rose. She finished the interview and had been called to wait for some time. Next was Rose; she came out of the interview room after half an hour.

"You took lot of time. Have you got selected?" Maria asked.

"No . . . Actually, the person was busy with his personal work," Rose betrayed.

"Oh, that's all right," Maria whispered.

All returned from Dubai to New York and back to their work. Rose informed the same thing to Payton as well about her interview.

Her family members weren't even mindful that she appeared in some interview. Rose was exultant after this interview because in reality, she was selected and had been offered to fly to Abu Dhabi in the United Arab Emirates.

Though she was blissful but muddled too. She knew the fact that if she would share her selection with her family, certainly they wouldn't permit her to go far. So she didn't share.

Nevertheless, she couldn't wait to inform her biggest accomplishment to Edward. Soon after returning from the Dubai, she called Edward after a long time and conceitedly informed him. Same as earlier, he didn't pay much attention to her and insouciantly hailed her.

Rose knows well that he won't permit her to go, but to envious him or to gain his concern for her she tried to take his attention.

Rose had seen a lot stages of her life in this short time. Nowadays, she was closer to Payton. All her leisure time passed with her.

She had turned out to be her mentor in some way. Whatever she said, Rose followed it.

Rose had moved ahead in her life, but she couldn't forget Edward. Whenever she passed with Payton through the Citi Financial branch, she always missed him. Her eyes always detected his car parked in front of the Citi Financial office.

It was going to be Christmastime; she had long December holidays. Her family had already ordered her to come soon. During this time, the hostel was going to be emptied as all the students returned back to their homes. Today, Rose, at her office, had to call some assigned data to her customer,

"Good morning. Can I speak to John?"

"No. Here, there is no John."

"Sorry, sir. I called the wrong number."

"Please don't put down the phone, please. If I'm not wrong, this is Rose speaking there."

"Um . . . Yes, may I know who's there?"

"Don't you remember, dear? This is Tom. What a lovely coincidence this is."

"Oops. Yaa, I remember. Right now, I'm in the office, and I need to put down the phone."

Rose tried to escape from this call. By mistake, she dialed the number that she never wanted to connect. When Rose came to this city, her first friend, Celestina, took her to visit Texas, her hometown. There, she met Tom.

He introduced himself as a married man to both. That's why Rose wasn't engrossed to talk to him. However, Tom was shrewd enough. He quest Rose's mobile number as he came to know about her office's name.

Rose's love life was critically devastated. She was no longer intent to make any male friends. Tom kept on calling Rose. As she didn't know his number, she accidentally picked his call.

"Please don't cut the phone. I just want to speak a few minutes. I need to clear the misunderstanding," Tom demanded.

"Okay! After that, don't call me again," Rose retorted.

"When we met earlier, I lied to you people just to get rid of your friend, Celestina, as she was bothering me. I'll be honest with you. I was never married, still single. If you don't believe me, you can come down to my city. I can prove it to you," Tom explained.

"Well, I don't need any proof. Let it be," Rose said irksomely.

Rose wasn't attracted to keep any relationship with any person as she was still committed to Edward despite all their fights.

After a month, Edward again called Rose and asked to conjoin sometime. Rose denied at first, but she couldn't resist seeing him. He had also shifted permanently to New Jersey. It was going to be vacation time, and Rose thought again to give a last chance to their relationship and finally sort out the things between them.

Without informing home, she left for New Jersey to meet him and surprise him on his birthday. She bought a beautiful sapphire shirt and large bouquets of red roses to gift Edward.

He received her, but this time, he stayed her at the hotel because of his family's presence. After a quarter, Rose met him. They had a wonderful dinner at five-star properties and spent the midnight time together.

Later, Edward left for home and came back in the morning to drop Rose at her hometown. Rose was going against all her near and dear ones to get Edward. She travelled this much only to charm him.

It seemed to her that her last night was wonderful. Now, she hoped for the best output. Christmastime was coming, and she was ready to rejoice with her family.

The moment she met Edward and returned to her place, she wanted to connect daily with Edward on the phone at least for a minute.

She wanted to celebrate the festival with him, but it never happened. Rose's one single text turned up Edward arrogant and not ready even to talk once.

This was a joyful time for Rose; her lifelong dreams were on the way. She received a post and confirmation letter about her selection in the Qatar Airways. Dates had arrived, and she needed to join next month.

She had been offered a handsome package of thirty thousand dollars annually. At the start of her career, Rose had made up her mind to leave for this, joining next month. She was successful in persuading her family as well. She returned from home after a majestic celebration and planned to give her resignation letter this week.

She hadn't yet disclosed it to anyone else except her family members. Luckily, Rose joined the office and was nearly done with the planning. She had written her resignation letter well to serve the notice period.

She informed the hostel authorities so that she got her deposit back. Payton was exultant for her friend, but at the same time, she was dejected as well to detach from her.

They started to do the packing for Rose as only few days were left for her to land in a new country.

Chapter 12

Three weeks later . . .

Rose put down her paper, wound off from the hostel, and readied to depart. Shopping was also completed. At 5:00 a.m., Rose was in deep slumber. Payton was sleeping beside her. Suddenly, she woke up.

Edward was calling.

Rose turned her cell to silent mode and went to sleep, thinking that he wouldn't call the next time. However, he kept on calling until she received the call.

"Hello," Rose whispered.

"You've always complained and fought with me. Now you'd be very happy. I'm admitted to the hospital," Edward stated.

"Oh! What are you saying? What happened to you?" Rose said, jittered.

"I'm getting operated for a back problem, and I have been suffering from kidney pain for a few months. But what to share with you?" Edward yelled.

"I'm sorry for all these things."

Early in the morning, Rose reached the hospital to visit Edward. His family members were with him, so Edward didn't allow it. Rose left his room in front of his family. She had to return to the hostel.

This incident had brought her in a confusing situation. She couldn't see her partner in such a condition. She was restless to meet him, but she couldn't even do that. One week later and Rose had done nothing but wait to meet him first. Frequently she had been calling him, but Edward didn't respond. Ten days later, Edward called Rose; it was just four more days for Rose to leave the city.

"Can I see you for the last time?" Edward craved.

"Yeah, where are you now?"

"Last night, I was discharged from the hospital. Now resting at home."

"Okay! I'll come at twelve p.m."

Rose left her work and went to see Edward. He was inclined in bed solos. As this was a weekday, all went to the office, and one servant was in the house to look after him.

Rose carried a beautiful bouquet of red roses with her and offered it to Edward with a love card with it. Rose, without waiting for anything, rushed to him and grabbed his arms.

She set down the stuff on the side table and sat beside Edward. Both leaned down on the bed; Rose was over Edward and snuggled closer to him.

Edward expressed his immense love for her. They took advantage of the desolate house and spent some of romantic moments.

Edward plunged in the romantic mood and held Rose tightly. He was over her, kissed on her forehead gradually cheek and neck.

"I love you. Please don't go anywhere. Don't leave me alone."

"I never wanted to leave you, but all the formalities are completed."

"It's in your hand. I want to marry you, and how'd I live here alone?"

"I also love you so much. Can do anything for you."

Romantic moments with Edward had made her again down to him and brought her closer to him once again.

She came back to the hostel and made up her mind to quit the idea of moving outside the country and stayed back in this place for him.

When Payton came to know this, she suggested, "Rose, don't drop the idea. This opportunity won't come again in your life."

Rose knew it, and still, her passion for aviation and flying were alive on the one side, but on the other hand, she couldn't detach from her partner. She wanted to be in the flying industry, and she could keep the commitment with her partner, but she feared to lose him.

Payton suspected Edward's movements and intentions for Rose. She wasn't even in favor of their relationship. However, she failed to induce her friend. At the end of their quarrel, Rose won it and wouldn't relocate. She first reached her office and wanted to cancel the notice period. She persuaded her director, but he wasn't ready to keep the contract with her anymore as someone else has been recruited in the place of the Rose.

She had no chance here; just fifteen days and her notice period would be completed. She was more fretful about her job and had already started applying for new ones.

She gave the notice period to the hostel also. Probably, after a fortnight, she wouldn't be having any accommodation. Edward was completely salubrious, and he left for New Jersey to join the office.

Rose wanted to seek his assistance for a job and accommodations. She probed him, "I'm looking out for a job urgently. If I need to survive here, I need a job. I won't be having any accommodation after this month. Can you help me with this?"

"At the moment, I'm busy. Will talk to you later," Edward said sketchily.

He didn't seem to be copious engrossed in Rose's problem. Once again, she was trapped. If she didn't get a job by the end of this month, she wouldn't be able to pay any expenses.

The next day at 7:00 p.m. . . . .

Office closing time while she return from office, when she came to know that one of her colleagues had gotten the offer from New Jersey for a counselor position, and the package was thrice Rose's current salary.

For her opulence her colleague didn't want to change the location because of her hometown.

She seized the opportunity and promptly applied for the job. This may have been her desire to follow Edward and spend as much time with him. Her recent application had been short-listed, and she had been offered a chance for a walk-in interview with the branch head.

This could be affirmative news for her, but presently, the challenge before her was to reach there unaccompanied as she couldn't stay there since she didn't know anyone out there. Furthermore, she couldn't afford to stay in any hotel even for a single day.

Trusting Edward wouldn't be a good idea for her as she had approached him, but he didn't take it seriously. Rose got wounded meditating on the behavior of her partner, which only existed for name's sake.

Once again, she needed Payton's counsels like earlier. "Why don't you seek Edward to go with you?" Payton asked.

"I've already asked him. He won't," Rose replied.

"Eh, in that case, at least you can demand him to book a private taxi for you, which accelerates you to travel and return on the same day," said Payton.

"Excellent! Thanks for the brilliant idea," Rose yelled.

"You're always welcome."

She got the arrangement for a private cab and attended the interview at daytime. By night, she contentedly returned to New York.

Edward received her at night in his car. He had booked the hotel for her as she wouldn't get an entry in her hostel, though she declined to drive with Edward. Payton facilitated for her to enter the hostel.

Rose somehow fathomed his intention; he chastely wanted to fulfill his needs. She was exhausted and had a bare stomach. Payton kept the food for her. Postdinner, she directly went to bed. Payton was blissful for her progression, but on the other hand, she didn't want to lose her first chum.

Rose later the last interview left for the training with her current organization as per the scheduled.

The moment Rose returned from the corporate training, she was offered the senior manager position at New Jersey and was obligated to join within two weeks.

Life had taken another turn for Rose. She was shuffling because of her partner Edward, but for her family and Payton evidence she is relocation for career opportunities.

Her psyche couldn't resist Edward. Rose had served the noticed period well and was ready for a new start. She called her father to aid her in shifting. In a very short duration, Payton and Rose had developed a very strong bond. Rose asked Payton to come down to New Jersey soon after completing her second year exams. Payton was also going to follow her friend.

All set, Rose joined her new office and was excited for this new city, but what disappointed her was the new accommodation.

She had booked the two-seater room and shared with a college girl but never chatted with her. The new staff members were virtuous. She missed her friend Payton badly. However, she had hopes alive that after three months, she'd also be coming to New Jersey.

Rose informed Edward on the very first day and insisted to meet him. She had no idea about him after their last meeting.

It'd been a month; she kept on texting him, continuously calling by mobile and landline number, but Edward hadn't exhibited any curiosity to meet her. It drove Rose to lose her rage. She had doubted him long back and caught him many times; despite this, she was ready to sort things out with him.

Today, while working in the afternoon, in the office, Rose tried to crack Edward's e-mail ID password, and she succeeded.

Whenever she called Edward at night, his phone was always engaged with some other network. Now they were in the same city; not only this, but their offices were also in the identical area.

Rose had sacrificed her career just for the sake of him. However, he barely bothered. Rose had decided to discover what was going on in his life.

She opened up his e-mail ID and was shocked to look at his chats. For a long time, Rose had been asking him for time and at least to introduce her to his family, but Edward had deceitfully escaped in the name of his career.

He acted critically when Rose asked him to meet.

Rose could see late-night chats with many girls in his list—most of them had a one-night relation with him. The rest were in his love list with whom he had been in regular touch since he proposed to Rose and started dating her.

This time, Rose was ready to burst on him and get rid of this relationship anyhow. She shared the matter with Payton; she suggested not having any contact with him if she wanted a happy life. Her elder sister also had the similar opinion about him. Rose was heated with him, and to some extent, these people persuaded her.

Weekend time and finally, Edward text her.

"Where are you?"

"Why do you want to know?" Rose said obscenely.

"I want to discuss something important."

"I don't have time. I'm in the office," Rose foully answered.

"When you get free, ring me. We'll go movie and discuss really important."

Rose was in the office now. She also missed true company in this city. Since she came here, no one even to talked to her. She had been sitting alone in the room after office hours.

Solitude had made her meet him once again, and the idea of watching a movie did not seem so bad. Apart from this, she had planned not to keep any kind of intimate relation with him further.

Before Rose could call him, he was waiting downstairs in the parked car.

They left for the movie theater near Rose's office. After watching the movie, Edward took her to his house.

Rose wanted to clarify many things with him, but he was busy watching football. Rose waited for him to talk, but when she saw that he wasn't intent to talk, she got off from the sofa and got ready to go out of the house. The moment she get off, Edward held her hand forcefully and graciously sat her back. He didn't let her go until he finished his game.

"What happened to you? Why are you showing me weird attitude?"

"I'm not," Rose urged.

"Let's forget, darling, all the past deeds, and begin a new relation."

"I'm no more intent to keep any relation with a person like you."

"What do you mean by that? A person like me?"

"I've seen your chat history. You're a manwhore hustler."

Edward lost his temperament and smacked her. Rose, without saying a single word, got off the bed and strode to the gate. She was no longer interested to talk or chat with him. Edward ran and grabbed her from behind and didn't allow her to move farther.

Forcibly, he brought her back to the room and pushed her to sit on the bed. She resisted a lot and jerked him, but she couldn't beat the physical strength of a man.

He held her hand without letting her move an inch.

"Please forgive me." He pretended to cry but without a single tear shedding.

Rose wasn't even bothered to hear him. She waited to get free from him and moved to her hostel. He touched Rose's hand and threw his hand to her breasts, but Rose jerked and didn't permit him to touch anywhere.

It took almost a day and a night until twelve. He kept on apologizing and finally succeeded at night. After a long fight, Rose was in his arms once again.

Slowly, he removed her top, gingerly touched her neck with his index fingertip, and kept on inkling her body. Rose was recumbent and naked in bed. She sensed the movement and had a pleasant smile on her face.

"Don't open your eyes for a while," he requested.

This statement made her suspicious about him, but to keep him pleased, she closed her eyes for a few minutes, and Edward was exploring all her curves. She felt weird but executed the order very well. After sex, Edward took a bath as always. He emanates from the bathroom and got engaged in watching television. She was sitting naked in bed, her back was against the wall, and suddenly, she picked Edward's mobile.

She glimpsed through it but was shocked to see a short video clip. She played the video again.

"What the hell is this, Edward?" Rose screamed.

He came beside her and held his phone. "Don't touch my mobile."

Rose hurriedly took his cell back and deleted the video.

"Why the hell did you make our sex video?" Rose breathlessly asked him.

"Yeah, I modestly wanted to keep the memory of our romantic moments."

Rose suspected him from the beginning.

Why do I trust this guy every time? she questioned herself. She agitatedly lay silently on the bed, her back opposite to Edward. The night was grim to pass. She qualms his intentions and could smell something bad. In the morning, at nine, Rose went back to her hostel to change and then joined the office as regular days.

Oh god, I've done the blunder of my life by trusting him, This thought kept juggling in her mind all the time.

She needed true companionship badly at this perilous stage to which she could share. However, her only friend, Payton, wasn't in this city, clueless of Rose's life. The thought whether he had deleted the pic or not kept on slaying her mind all the time.

In the evening, at half past eight, Rose was sedentary in her room and found it difficult to even breathe coolly and upturned when Tom started calling her frequently. Tom explicitly shared the entire about him. He was a successful entrepreneur of Britain who owned a steel company. He adulated Rose from the first day of their casual meeting. Unfortunately, Rose couldn't imagine anyone else but Edward.

Despite all the cruel behavior of her partner, she stuck on her decision to be with him.

Anglie was right. Why did I move ahead with Edward? Rose questioned herself after all the wrong with her love relationship.

One month after that unforgettable night . . .

Rose couldn't forget the devious Edward. She had made up her mind: either she'd get married to him only or stay single.

After that murky night, Rose was waiting for her menstruation. As she suspected the intention of him, he didn't use precaution that night. He skipped by excusing, "Don't worry, I won't insert deep."

Rose wanted to delete the biggest mistake of her life and didn't want to trust anyone else in this world. It'd been more than a month, and she didn't menstruate. Rose was sure of her pregnancy but wanted to confirm this with the GP.

After returning from the office, she directly reached to consult her GP. After having a couple of tests, her pregnancy was confirmed by the GP.

Worried, she returned to the hostel, buried her head under the pillow, and wept the entire night. She couldn't even cry piercingly as her other roommate was studying.

At this vilest moment, she was unaccompanied in this city. Payton was at New York one more month for her to arrive in this city. She couldn't disclose it to her family members.

One month ago, Tom had taken too much attention in her life and persistently presaged her to stay away from Edward.

"He's an oversexed male with the least respect for women."

Rose recalled this statement of Tom's. Nothing could be done now but to face it unaided. Tom requested her countless times to call him whenever she was free, but she barely texted him.

She couldn't emanate with the fear of Edward. The fact in her mind was to tell Edward about her pregnancy. She was sure that he wouldn't comfort her in any way, but she still thought, somehow, he might have a soft corner for his child.

She never desired to talk with the devious person ever in her life, but the situation had made her again gather courage and at least inform him about his child.

She didn't have many options except to get married to Edward. She swiftly dialed his number.

"Edward, I need to meet you urgently, please."

"I don't have time. I'll talk to you later." Edward abruptly disconnected the phone.

Rose was destitute as she couldn't go anywhere after three months. If she'd take maternity leave, then she wouldn't survive as she was absolutely dependent on the job. Rose kept aside her dignity and continued calling for the child's sake.

"Why the hell do you call me repetitively? Don't disturb me. I'm a busy man," he yelled.

"I won't disturb you in the future again, Edward. I'm pregnant. It's our child. Will you give your name to our child?" Rose begged for the unborn child.

"No, never. Have you gone insane? I don't know whose child that is. Never call me again, you slut," he responded bluntly and kept the phone.

Life had been never disappointing before this time. She couldn't get a single day off from the office as she was still on probation period and training wasn't yet completed. Neither her family nor Payton knew.

Why did I meet him? Why did I trust him? All my well-wishers were right. He's a hustler, bankrupt with the emotion, Rose asked herself. *Oh, Lord! I've lost my career, myself. How will I face my family now? Where would I go?* Rose complained to God for her sufferings.

In this blackest time of her life, Tom proposed to her; all she could do was to reject his proposal. She couldn't divulge to Tom that she was pregnant with Edward's child.

No one will accept me now, then why would Tom? Rose said to herself.

Tom was a smart young business tycoon. He suspected Rose in their chats and forced her to be explicit with him. He kept reciting about Edward's nature and his starvation for girls; he also presaged her to stay away from that person.

In these few days, he utilized his social networking, investigated all about his past, and established that Edward was the most loose male character he had ever come in touch with. Not only to Rose he's cheating, but there were many girls who had been his victims.

You're too late. Nothing can be done now, and you should have informed me earlier, Rose thought in her mind but couldn't reveal to Tom.

Tom loved Rose devoid of even meeting her. They met just once, and now, he was ready to marry her. Exam date came for the final year exams; Rose started packing her baggage.

She can't deny at home not to come otherwise they'll whiff the unpleasant. She had completed the three months in her new profile, and the branch manager agreed to sanction her two weeks leave just because of Rose's performance in the office.

Rose was one and half months pregnant, but she didn't know what to do with this. If she tried contacting her GP, it'll take her no less than two months' time for the abortion procedure. She wanted to keep the baby, but when she looked at the future, she thought to abort it.

Neither to perform the abortion she has time nor money to go for private consultation, as her two-month salary was due to be credited. She was blank as to what to do with her life, for her life had finished.

Forlornly, she reached her hometown for the exams. Things were no more like before in her life before.

Rose's mom and sister worried, scrutinizing the tension in her eyes. Her face was dull, and she hardly gathered with the family and chatted with anyone. She hadn't studied anything this year and was sure to fail in all the exams.

On June 1, 2008, Payton was about to arrive at New Jersey as planned by them earlier. Two weeks more to go, she had taken the transfer from New York to New Jersey just for the sake of her only chum.

During the last quarter, the empathy between the two wasn't as before. Tom emerged as a new mentor in Rose's life. Lack of communication from Rose's side had built the distance between the two friends.

Before relocating to this place, Rose stanch to Payton when she would go there. They would shift together, but last month, they had been fighting on the timing issues.

Last month, Rose was occupied with her new job. While after office hours, she was on the phone with Tom. This had created enough distance.

While Rose was at home, Payton was angry with her for not supporting her in relocating as she was going to there for her sake.

Though Rose had been waiting for her for a long time.

Payton called her several times and requested her help for the shifting, but since last month, Rose's life had outrageously grieved at its worst.

June 21, 2008.

"Why aren't you picking up my call?" Rose asked furiously.

"Say, why are you calling?" Payton rudely answers.

"Please, I'm sorry, Payton. I know I can't justify with our relation and didn't keep the commitment as we planned, but please, there is nothing left for me in my life," Rose entreated, sobbing.

"What? Say it again. What's wrong with you? Please share with me." Payton suspected her long back. Perhaps she had a clue but wanted Rose to share with her.

"Please, Payton, don't leave me at this time. I beg, please," Rose beseeched for her support.

"Yeah, I know you're hiding something from me. I'll feel better if you'd tell me." She was pretty sure that she had some problems with Edward.

"Come here with me. I'll tell you later. First, promise me you'll shift with me in the same apartment." Rose pursued her at her best.

"Yes, I'll be going there next week." Payton's anger didn't last much on her; even she didn't want to go anywhere else leaving Rose.

Rose would be joining Payton after three weeks, soon after her exams. She was sure to fail in all the exams.

This time, Anglie bluntly asked Rose about her love affair. She asked her whether she had some physical relation with him or not. She kept on marking the same thing to her, but Rose wouldn't share with her. Anglie grumbled about her nature as well; according to her, she had transformed entirely.

She could watch her apathetic to her surroundings. All these hints forced Anglie to believe more about Edward and Rose's love relations.

She had been caring for her since her childhood. All she could do was to warn her. Nothing else she could do with her. Three weeks after, Rose joined the office. The very first day, she visited the GP after office hours. She wanted to abort finally.

She alleged to take pills and be terminated, but the GP disapproved it.

"You're too late for the pills, Rose. Only one month pregnancy can be aborted with pills. You're going be three months pregnant, and you need to have surgery."

"Okay, what will it cost me?" Rose asked a little worriedly.

"Well! You must know, as this is too late, it'll cost you a bit higher—around about four thousand dollars," the GP answered.

"Proceed with it. How much time will it take?" Rose investigated.

"An hour, but it'll take a week for you to recover." The GP suggested for her to take a rest after the operation.

"Please do it, Doctor, urgently."

"Sure, that's my job. Anyways, who will accompany you during the time of operation?" The GP wanted someone to take care of her after the operation.

"Why, Doctor? There's no one. Is it possible that I can go after the operation back to my room?"

Rose didn't have anyone to even look after her. Payton came in this city, but she hadn't shared anything with her. Just for one month, she was living with her aunt and would join her after a few weeks.

"Well, normally we don't discharge anyone on the same day as subsequent to surgery, immense bleeding takes place that lasts for a week. You'd be given the anesthesia, and in that condition, no one is conscious even to stand, and you're talking about discharge?" The GP suggested she not get an immediate discharge after surgery as she's sure it'll be risky.

"Please, Doctor, I won't be able to stay here. The next day I need to attend the seminar and give a really important presentation that can't be cancelled."

It extended to almost three months because Rose was lacking the funds. Today, her salary was credited for the last two months. She did not even inform her friend Payton about her situation.

Although she took her to the hospital where she consulted the private doctor, she had been waiting outside discerning that Rose was discussing some general health problems.

One Sunday afternoon, agitatedly, Rose reached the hospital by private taxi, nervous for her first operation in life. If something went wrong, there was no one to look after her.

The doctor transported her to the operation lab. As she came unaided, that wasn't permitted. She was supposed to come with her partner or fiancé. Rose mentioned to the doctor. She took her to a private ward that was not accessible to the common person.

The doctor gave her anesthesia to proceed further for the surgery. Rose was scared even too inclined down and get ready for the operation; prior to this she hadn't been injected.

"Dear, please try to cooperate. I assure you you won't feel pain. You need to trust me. This isn't my first time, and everything will be all right soon," the GP solaced.

She injected her and completed the surgery in a private ward. Rose gets consciousness after an hour. Due to the operation, she had a huge blood loss, and it made her scrawny even to stand on her own.

"Congrats! All done safely. Hopefully, you will recover in a week. I've prescribed you pills to take for a month, and all the blood loss will be same as before. Try to get as much juice as possible," the doctor recommended.

"Please, Doctor, drop me at my room. I need to go to the office and give an important presentation," Rose entreated.

The doctor recommended her to drink some juice, but Rose didn't take anything after surgery. The doctor dropped her at her room, but she didn't even have the endurance to get off from the bed and move upstairs for dinner. Rose awoke late at night because of thirst, but there was no one in the room to get her some water. At nine in the morning, she got ready for the office. If she didn't go, then it'd be difficult for her to continue in the company.

"Oh, God! Give me strength to wake up and stand," Rose implored in fear for the sake of her survival.

Today, she had an important presentation at the office. She needed to stand at least for two hours. Grim life presently, but she kept moving.

Two weeks later . . .

Rose and Payton discovered a place to live together. They had been stiffly searching for one month. During her pregnancy time as well, Rose went with Payton and searched one by one for room options by knocking on every single door.

Like Rose, Payton also couldn't afford to hire any private cab or travel by tube. Her condition was scantier than Rose as she had never worked before. Payton perceived a solemn distress on her face.

She asked her numerous times, but Rose didn't disclose a single word. She continued repeating, "This isn't the right time to discuss. I don't know why you suspect me. I'm not smacking anything to you," She feared to lose Payton if she'd disclose it to her. Inside, she felt her actions were wrong and she did a sin.

However, the very first day they shifted, they quarreled as Rose wasn't the same as before for Payton. She no longer provided time for Payton, and after returning from the office, she simply sat alone or talked on the phone with Tom.

Payton was oblivious to the drastic situation with which Rose was going through. All she needed was her friend back in the normal life again. She wanted to see Rose happy, same as three months ago.

A fortnight was over since her operation. Mentally, she hadn't convalesce from the pregnancy shock, and life was not ready to bring the virtuous for her yet.

She tried to focus just purely on her career to earn for her survival and had dropped the idea of marriage forever.

At twelve in the afternoon, Rose was at the office, replying to official mails. Suddenly, she logged into her personal Yahoo! ID. She gasped to see the unanticipated mail from Edward: "Call me." Her love for Edward had converted into abhorrence after such a painful time for her that she could never forget in her life. She shunned the mail and firm never ever to see him or talk.

The next day, she got a call from Edward. Again she neither picked up nor replied anything. She'd been neutral for him now to avoid further hitches. Edward was the major problem in her life; additionally, her professional carrier had also ended because of him

On weekends, Rose was with Payton at the shopping mall. She took her forcibly to cheer her.

This was their first day in New Jersey, which was ruined when Edward called her, and once again, she didn't pick up. Later, she received a text form him: "Don't try to avoid me. It'd be dangerous for you. Call me as soon as possible." Hazardously, she took Payton back to their flat.

"What happened? What's this? Why do you look hassled and didn't utter a single word? Is there something wrong?"

"Nothing's wrong. All's fine."

"Don't dupe me. I know you very well. You can't hide from me." Payton assuredly probed.

"Please let me sleep now. I'm feeling tired." Rose strained to escape from Payton's questions.

Edward's text dismayed her enough that she couldn't sleep. The whole night, her mind kept on wondering the ways to escape from him. He presaged Rose to contact him before next week, but Rose didn't follow. Next week, Edward mailed again.

"If you won't call me before the evening today, I'll upload your video on the Internet."

Confounded, she immediately shut her mail so that others can't watch her. She had not overcome from the surgery, and again, Edward started bothering her. Vulnerably, she came back to the flat, and late that night, she gave a missed call to Edward. He didn't call today, but the succeeding afternoon, he called.

"Why weren't you responding to my calls and mails?"

"I wasn't in the city and went for training," horrendously she replied, trying to stay away from him and remain safe.

She was aware of Edward's political background and good networks in politics. She couldn't face all this alone.

Rose came from a lower middle-class family. Her father was just an accountant, and her mother was a teacher. She lacked the social networking. Edward ordered her to meet him in a couple of days. He was about to reach New Jersey next week.

Rose didn't find any option other than to do whatever he said. She understood this man had never loved her but embittered her in the name of marriage and sexually exploited her.

It was too late for her realization. If she'd listened to all her near and dear ones, she wouldn't have been in such shit. She didn't do anything wrong in her point of view because loving someone blindly wasn't a crime.

Payton had been surveilling her activities during midnight. She went out of the room into the bathroom when the phone rang to talk to someone, and after a few minutes' talk, she came back. Since they had been in relationship, they never went alone without informing each other. Subsequently, after office hours, Rose clandestinely went outside to meet someone. This made Payton question her, "Where are you going? I also want to accompany you."

She changed her clothes. "Please let me go, Payton. I know I'm not justifying with our relationship, but please, try to understand me. I can't take you with me." Rose escaped from further questions.

This continued for a few days. Today, they went outside for entertainment and some fun. While taking lunch, Rose was frightened. Her eyes kept roaming around like not to catch by someone. Her physical presence with Payton and mental absence increased her disbelief to surety. She was annoyed enough with Rose.

"If you think I'm your friend, then you've to disclose the truth," Payton cautioned.

"I can't say here. Let's go home. Even I want to confess." Rose gave her acceptance.

Rose closed the door and pushed Payton on the bed and demanded, "Before I reveal, promise me, Payton, you'll never share the truth with anyone else."

"Trust me, I will never disclose to anyone. Not even my would-be," she vowed.

"When you weren't here, I met Edward, just once. I tried my best to retain him. One haunting night, we crossed the limits and had gone out of control. I wasn't conscious that time, and he took advantage and had made my two-minute video clip during sex. He made me pregnant, and now he is blackmailing me." She shared the biggest truth of her life, which killed her every moment.

"Aw, I'm sorry for my behavior for the last few days. Why haven't you shared all this before if you have trusted me? I always wished to stand beside you in your entire struggle. Don't worry, dear. Whatever you plan for the future, I'm with you," Payton guaranteed.

Rose burst into tears in the arms of Payton and felt a bit relaxed after spitting all the bitter truth.

"That's the reason, despite my aversion, I need to talk to him whenever he calls. Now you tell me, what should I do?" she said despondently, seeking for Payton's suggestion.

"Now you aren't alone. I'm with you. He has exploited you enough. You'll neither meet him nor talk to him," Payton suggested assuredly.

"Are you crazy? If I won't reply to him, then he'll spread my videos!" she roared.

"I'm sure if you'll go on following him, then there wouldn't be the end of this. He'll keep exploiting whenever he needs. Better you face it once, and after that, he won't have anything to blackmail you with" startlingly Payton suggested though it was difficult for Rose to follow.

She gave thought to Payton's interpretation and concluded that she was right. If she would flout him, probably, it would be the best option.

One month later . . .

Rose's life was moving on. She was no longer vexed about Edward's admonitions and kept on shunning him.

She had been not so closer to Payton before this. Her hard time had brought her in an intimate relationship with her. Rose wished to continue with the same company, but the circumstances didn't allow her to do so.

She had never settled in her personal life, so professionally, she wanted to settle. However, this wasn't happening.

In the past half year, she had developed a decent bonding with her colleagues and branch managers, but recently, the old staff had been replaced by their branch.

She was the only one who didn't find other job opportunities. Frantically, she was in search to enter the aviation sector, but time had vanished. She got calls neither from airlines nor from any educational establishments.

Payton had quite settled in a new place. Her college was not going well, but her professional life had taken a good start. Her situation was also similar to Rose. To survive there in a more expensive city than their previous one, she had to work part-time while studying.

Whenever Payton comprehends Rose, she noticed a zeal, thrust for the partner. She was unable to make any decision. Further, her past incidents had made her a bit rigid girl.

Rose didn't notice Tom's love for her; he proposed to her long before and had been in regular touch with her on the phone.

He always requested her to leave a text so that whenever she was free, he could contact her. Habitually, he called her daily after working hours before seeking her permission.

"Rose, please move ahead in life. Edward was never yours and won't be in the future. You deserve a better partner," Payton solaced.

"I can't forget him. I've decided never to get married with anyone. If I want to then also no one will accept me with this past. I'm sure Edward will create a problem for me," Rose glumly expressed.

"It's not like that. You failed to choose the right person. Not all the people are like your first love. Have credence in relationships. Maybe God has made someone exceptional for you, who's yet to arrive in your life or probably entered but you couldn't see him," Payton said, being diplomatic.

"What can't I see? What are you talking about?" Rose probed cynically.

"If you couldn't get your love, that doesn't mean no one should get their love. I've been perceiving that Tom cares for you a lot, but you never bothered about him. Spend time with him steadily. You'll start feeling better."

"He's a good human being, that much I know, but I can't love anyone else than Edward."

"Oh, it's more important you adore him. And never forget, if you want to be happy, marry a person who loves you, not you love him."

"Huh–uh."

"If you don't love him, that's reasonable, but you respect him. By the time you start spending time with him, inevitably, you'll fall in love with him." Payton pleasantly counseled her best friend.

Though she wasn't in favor of Edward since the beginning of Rose's relationship, she was slightly positive for Tom.

"Thanks for your emotional support. I think you're right," Rose nodded.

She got a new hope to live life. Following her friend's suggestions, nowadays, she texted Tom regularly. Soon, after coming from the office, Tom never called her without her permission. Their conversations would last until late at night.

Tom was a rich male. He was occupied with ample meetings at daytime, but he kept the nighttime for Rose daily.

Rose had met him once only when Tom saw her with Celestina but never had any personal meeting.

From his side, he was ready to marry anytime and wished to introduce Rose to his family as soon as possible. However, Rose hadn't accepted his proposal. It was not because of her love for Edward but fear of him.

She qualmed, if Tom would know her past, then, probably, he'd leave her undeniably. Tom explained to her everything regarding his past and present life, but he never got any clear answers from Rose's side. He wished her to unclutter herself in front of him.

Contrary to this, Tom was stingy about her, as she and Edward lived in the same city and he lived in another.

"Rose, please, if you don't mind, just once, I want to meet you. I can land the next day if you allow me." Tom sought permission.

He saw her two years ago. He promised her once she accepted his proposal for marriage that she didn't need to distress anyone in the world. Tom used all his contacts to identify Rose's life. He figured out Rose's past life almost through his nearby friends who were in touch with Edward.

"I request you, Rose. If you don't say yes to me, that's fine, but never turn back to your ex-love. He's damn shit who has exploited so many girls. You're lucky you were saved and, at the right time, you escaped from his conspiracy," He countered his views toward Edward. Indirectly, he restraints Rose and wanted her to confess her past life in front of him.

You don't know, Tom. I'm also a victim of his, and I wasn't saved but badly trapped. Once you'll come to know about my life, then you won't be able to love me anymore, Rose said to herself. She actually wanted to reveal it to him.

Today, Rose left from the office early and got ready to receive Tom as they were going to meet for the first time after they were committed to each other. She dressed in seductive pink with high heels and light makeup. They came to the city mall, and Tom couldn't hold his gaze on her model-like personality. He was not seductive for Rose as Edward was, but gradually, she had developed a soft corner for him.

He wore a simple basic T-shirt and blue denims with shades. He was six feet tall and had a dusky complexion with a black curled hair.

They dined in a five-star hotel, and Rose appealed for him to drop her to the flat soon because Payton was waiting for her. He dropped her, but he requested Rose to stay connected with him the entire night while he might be travelling back to his hometown.

It had been a month for Rose; Edward hadn't troubled her. She desired he should move ahead in his life with anyone. Rose lately switched a job and made up her mind to accept Tom's proposal today night.

She returned from the office and desperately waited for the call, which she had never felt before. Another reason for accepting Tom's proposal was she found it difficult to struggle alone. Not only this, she loved Edward a lot, but she had never spent such time with him over the phone just the way like Tom cared for her.

At midnight, Rose made him dumbstruck.

"Please say it one more time for my sake. You love me?" he requested.

"Yes, I do."

It was too late Tom and Rose will have an office tomorrow. They kept their phones down and chose to meet at the latest. Valentine's Day was approaching soon.

Rose's life wasn't utterly smooth, but she had at least recovered from the Edward terror. If Payton wouldn't have solaced her at the right time, Edward would have exploited her completely.

On February 14, 2009, Tom called her in the afternoon.

"Happy Valentine's Day. I love you so much. I'm waiting for you at the Hilton hotel tonight at nine. Would you join me?" he surprised Rose.

The unanticipated visit had brought a blush on her face after a long. This would be her second Valentine's Day celebration.

Tom gifted her a delicate round–shaped dial watch that had all the colors and a bunch of red roses paired with an attractively handwritten greeting card. Propitiously, she returned home after such a wonderful night.

In the morning at nine, Rose and Payton started packing for their official trip to Dubai. They were employed with the same company.

Rose hadn't informed her touring to Tom, dreading that if she divulged it, he may possibly force to meet her because he'd also be leaving for it the day after.

She had a general chat with him in the morning at ten. Now, she was in the air, Payton was sitting beside her seat, and their boss sat facing them.

Suddenly Rose was alerted; her cell rang, which was expected, from her side, but she couldn't pick up. Tom kept on calling her at sundry times. She thought it wouldn't be a good idea to talk in front of the boss. If she wouldn't talk for one day, nothing will come to harm.

Instantly, she dropped a message, stating to talk tomorrow. Tom didn't understand and was ignorant of her situation; he called nearly fifty times but got no response. After texting him, she kept the phone inside the bag.

In addition, the three went to sleep. The next day, early in the morning, she got occupied with the official work. Her director boss was accompanying her all the time. They left for the hotel accommodation, where they freshened up and got ready for the meetings. The entire day, they didn't get a single minute.

They took food at eleven that night. Tom had been piqued. In the morning, he started calling repetitively without perturbing anything, even though he called Rose's office landline number. From there he acquired her official mobile number, given by the company, and shortly, he called all the possible options.

He had even called her mother too.

He was not going to stop; he dialed Rose's official mobile number. "Rose, why are you not picking up the call?" he said animatedly. He didn't even bother to know who was there on the other side.

"Yes, please, this is a Mr. Jackson on line. She's interviewing."

At twilight, while Rose assembled with the boss to converse for next day's plans, she learned that Tom had called her number and that the entire day he called like hell.

153

"Payton, what's wrong with him? Can't he wait just one day?" Rose shrieked.

"I don't know what happened to him. Probably, he's thwarted as we didn't reveal to him our touring," Payton enigmatically replied.

At half past twelve, Rose called Tom.

"You cheated on me. You broke my trust. I was planning to marry you by the end of this year, and you've shown me your real colors." He sounded mad to Rose as she has no idea what he was talking about.

"When did I cheat on you? How did I break your trust?"

"You lied to me. You never informed me that you're going to Dubai for a day. Last month, you and Edward were together in a one hotel," Tom accused Rose without asking for the reality.

She was speechless, but her mind was in such a fuming mood, she screamed, "If you don't know anything, then don't blame. Mind your words before you speak."

"I know what I spoke. I'm right. Now, I'll never trust you. You used me." He clarified his words. "Not only this, you weren't responding to my calls because you were with the boss in a hotel. Now I can understand how you move ahead in your career at this early stage," he impugned.

Rose had no impression how he came to know and how he'd turned up so rude overnight.

"You've shown me your dirty thinking. I didn't tell you because I've arrived here for couple of days, and yes, I was with him, but that time, I was committed to him and not to you," she elucidated.

"Aw, finally you accepted the truth. I just wanted to hear this, and I've recorded all your conversation as a proof." He made Rose accept her past, which she never wanted to recall again in her life.

"Thank God! Edward saved me at the right time. If he hadn't called me yesterday and exposed to me all the things then I'd have been exploited by you. But thanks to him, he's my godfather." He disclosed the truth behind his behavior. Edward had molded his mind in a day.

"I warned you to never chat with him and stay away from him. If you'd have loved me, then you would have never chatted with him," Rose indicated.

She couldn't imagine in her life as took a long time to ponder anyone else then Edward, though Payton convinced her she moves further.

"Look at this, Payton. I was scared of this situation. Tom had proved himself to me. He doesn't even bother to ask me the truth," she said awfully.

"Please forget this, darling. At least it's good you haven't planned your life with him. Otherwise, this would have resulted in divorce," said Payton.

"Huh-uh. What to do with this recording? I can whiff his intentions aren't good. He also wrought like Edward," Rose quandaried.

"Damn, I remember enough with these guys. You just relax. We can't do anything now, but we've to wait for their activities."

Probably, this was her last talk to Tom. She wanted to move ahead with him and was sustaining her fidelity for him, but if she would talk to him further, then again, he could record all their conversations.

They returned from the tour and went back to the office. Her love drove her humiliated enough in front of her director.

Now, when Rose had stopped picking up his calls on mobile, he started calling her on the office landline. Rose wanted neither Edward nor Tom. She was in search of peace. She had started feeling like the crime she did was loving in her life.

Rose's personal life was never good. Ever since she had fallen in love with her first boss, since then her life had been hell.

One week later . . .

Rose took a medical leave to visit her father, who was not well. Payton also accompanied her as her father had a severe heart attack.

All the family members of Rose were in the hospital.

When they returned from the hospital, her father was resting and her mother was with her father. Alarmingly, their landline phone kept on ringing.

First, no one picked up as all the family members were using mobiles, so no one usually called at this number. At daytime, they evaded the phone, but at 1:00 a.m., the phone rang repetitively. It was kept there in the parents' room.

Her mother picked the call. "Please don't keep the phone. I want to share with you regarding Rose," said Tom.

"This isn't the right time," Mom stated and kept the phone. The next day, early in the morning, he started calling again, and her mother was outside the home. Rose saw the number and unplugged the cable.

She tried to avoid these people as long as she could. Payton also suggested to her to change her personal number.

Tom didn't seem to stop at this. He now started calling Payton, and she had also saved his number and didn't pick the call. They feared if they picked up once again, he would make the recording and could use it against them.

A few days later, Rose checked her mails. She could see a mail from Tom,

"Please talk to me, just once. I won't trouble you, I swear. Please. Love you so much."

Rose didn't respond. This person had made her life hell. She never projected a single night skipped talk could trouble her.

Not only she but Payton had also not reverted anything to him.

"Payton, we need to find a solution to get rid of this person. We can't change our phone numbers every time," Rose furiously said.

"Let us go back to our office, then we can work it out. We can't do anything from home."

Her father was recuperating now, and they went back for their work. While Rose returned to her office, her branch manager wanted to meet her immediately.

"Yes, ma'am!"

"How's your father now?" the manager questioned.

"He's recovering."

"I'm sorry, Rose, but you can't continue with this company anymore," the manager detested.

"What's the reason, ma'am?"

"It's been a week. Continuously, we're been receiving a call from an unknown person saying nuisance about you. He has called numerous times and also cautioned us that he can come down to our office," explained the manager.

"Yes, I'll resign today itself."

Oblivious to what the manager was talking about, she could figure only either Edward or Tom had done this act. Previously, she was absconding from Edward, and now, both were organized. She had lost the job when she was about to be promoted.

No airline was open to her. She had difficulty finding a job. She came back from the office but kept on pondering about the phone call. *Who's that guy? What all he disclosed to the manger?* Rose probed herself. She contemplated to query further and approached a front office colleague who was also a good friend of hers.

"Sara, Rose here. Can you do me a favor?" Rose requested.

"Yes, ma'am," her colleague replied.

"You must be aware that I resigned from the office. As you sit at the front desk and receive all the calls first, please tell me, who was the person, and what did he say?"

"Well, he didn't divulge his name. The code from that number was from New York. He kept repeating about MMS and some videos of yours. I know this much only," Sara formally educated.

"Thanks for the details. Bye."

Rose was sure about this. She could assume that this could be no one than Edward as he had her video. She qualms Edward may have spread her video all around. At evening time, Payton returned from the office.

"I've lost my job. Edward had spread my video at the office," Rose said with loathing.

"Shit, he's such a bastard," Payton accused him. Rose couldn't stop her tears. Gloomily, she fell into Payton's arms and wept. There were no more hopes alive her for life.

"Payton, I won't be able to face my parents. What would I do if this video reached them?"

"Aw . . ."

"I request you, if ever you find me dead, then never let my parents know the reason behind it. I don't want to embarrass them," Rose said with despise.

"Don't talk rubbish. Everything will be all right soon. If you'd lose hope, then what about your family, darling? I'm with you always," Payton said pitifully. Rose was grateful to Payton for her support during the last few years.

"Before it reaches your home, ask Anglie to take care of the phone calls and change the settings of your mother's cell phone," Payton shrewdly advised.

Rose instructed, "Anglie, please do me a favor. Please check our mother's cell phone whether she has her smartphone settings activated, and also, take care of the landline phone. Tom shouldn't talk to her."

"Okay, but it's difficult as I've an exam in a week, but I'd take care of it," Anglie assured.

Rose continued to undergo distressing situations. Previously, she used to have a job; presently it was difficult for her even to stay in the same city.

She was oblivious which were all the places Edward had spread the videos, but she suspected, probably, he had handed it over to Tom. Rose stopped going out anywhere. Both Payton and Rose started searching for new accommodations.

Rose wasn't ready to go out anywhere out of the room. At the flat itself, she didn't even move out of the room so that no one couldn't detect her.

"Why aren't you moving out? See, nothing will happen merely sitting in a room. Don't fear much." Payton questioned.

"Please take me out somewhere else. I don't want to stay in this city anymore. Every second can't live in terror," Rose roared.

"Eh, we'll plan. We don't have any contacts outside. How can we relocate? And our family members also can't support us. Wait for a couple of months. Let us make some savings," Payton propagated.

Rose horrendously started searching for a job; she contacted all the agencies, hoping for the best. Month end both left with little dosh.

Rose's last month salary was due, and she was unsure whether she was going to receive it or not. She hadn't informed her family members that she lost her job. A few days to go for the rent. Whatever saving she had done was disbursed in the abortion.

"Don't worry! This month I've the savings. I can bear the rent for both," Payton committed.

"Thanks you so much."

For a month, Rose didn't move out of the home. She kept on applying for a job by herself. Payton had decided to take Rose out and take the fear out of her. Surprisingly, she booked a movie ticket for both.

She was successful, but the entire way, she seemed to be hiding from the crowd. However, Payton hoped she'd make her out of hell.

As Rose had no work, she passed her time on Payton's laptop, playing games. She quite enjoyed it for the first time. By the way, she had buried sundry torments inside but pretended to be cheerier.

These days, Tom came to visit Switzerland and European countries to chill out.

He kept on mailing and texting her through their number. They avoided it, but their mail ID was still the same.

At 3:00 p.m., Rose's mother was at home. Frustratingly, she has picked the call, which rang ten times.

"Hello, Auntie, please give me just ten minutes. This is something very urgent about Rose," Tom probed.

"How do you know my daughter?" Mom confirmed.

"I've known her for two years. I love her so much, and we have spent quality time together," Tom revealed.

"I don't trust you."

"I know that. I've done her audio recording. You can listen to it. If you want, I can provide you the snaps as well as a proof."

"Yes proof me?" Mom jiggled.

Tom connected the recording, which he made some days ago. Not only this, he had done Payton's recording as well. He made her listen to both.

"I hope now you believe me. I know you work at a college as a professor. Your husband is retired as an accountant. Anglie, Rose's elder sister, is doing pharmacy . . ."

"Oh . . ."

"Mom, come here soon. Someone's urgently calling you." Anglie cunningly diverted her mom's mind and disconnected the phone. Later, she instantly informed it to Rose.

"Do you know how much he said?" Rose keenly inquired.

"No, I don't know. By the time I arrived, Mom was listening to him. She's going to ask you all now. Be prepared," said Anglie.

"Yeah."

"Anglie, call Rose and give me the phone." Mother ordered.

"What are you doing, Rose? Your friend called us today that you were going with him. Last week, you were with him. How does he know all about our family?" Mom said heatedly.

160

"Mom, please, right now I'm at the office. I'll talk to you in the evening," Rose conned.

"Call me in the evening, definitely," Mother ordered.

"Yes, sure . . ."

Rose absconded from the replies temporarily, thinking that she may be prepared with all the answers later. She planned to discuss with Anglie and Payton, then she'd chat with her mother.

Early in the evening, she called Anglie.

"What was their conversation?" Unfortunately, Anglie knew a portion of it.

"He shared some telephonic conversation of yours and Payton's, which talks about your relation with him. You were with him at a New York hotel. You're in shit with wily Edward," Anglie divulged, repeating her mother's word.

"Thanks, Anglie. Please keep watch over her. Make sure she doesn't pick the call next time, please," Rose requested.

"You haven't shared anything with me. Tell me the truth. What are you people doing out there?" Anglie yelled.

"I'll tell you the integral thing in detail later. Please save me now," Rose asked for the favor.

"Okay, don't worry. I'll try to handle it."

Rose quaked to hear that he had made the Payton recording as well. Even after talking at once. She didn't have a full idea, but she could figure out the intentions of these two people.

She feared the video; it shouldn't reach her parents anyhow.

Problems kept on growing. Rose found the best solution for it was to better vanish from the world. Every second of her life passed by speculating the actions of her two lovers who had merged to destroy her.

There was neither a private life nor a professional, despite money problems, no accommodations to live from next month, every moment tension surrounded either there heart breaking phone call, threating mails.

"Rose, Tom and Edward are doing this because they can no longer use you now. If we want to get rid of these people, probably, we can talk to him for the last time. Maybe something can be sorted out," Payton suggested.

"What if he again records my conversation?" Rose asked.

"Do one thing: drop him a mail. Till the time we don't find any job accommodation for us, you can chat with him ominously. This is the last option we have."

"I hope it works. Otherwise, I've no hopes left. If my parents will come to know, I'll die."

"Please be positive."

The next day, Rose dropped a mail to Tom.

"What is left between us, for that you keep on calling my home and me if you think this is the way you'll get me then you won't."

She was bankrupted of feelings and no more desired these people as her life partner—not even as a person to have any kind of contact with.

"Please, once, pick my call. I promise I'll never bother you. I love you so much," Tom mailed her.

Rose picked his call and asked, "I no more trust you. Whatever you want to say, say it from the STD or from the landline so that you may not record."

He calls her form the nearby STD, "Thanks for allotting me the time. I'm sorry, Rose, if you're angry with me, but I did right. I wanted you to undergo the pain that I've gone through," Tom delicately blamed.

"You're such a cheap person I can ever think of. You were the same person who promised, 'I'll be with you till the last breath. Never hurt you.' Will stand with me in all the problems. Not only this, never do anything without my permission. What I hurt you? Damn! Just a single night I didn't pick the call, and you showed me your true colors," Rose screamed.

"I promised you, I remember, but you cheated on me. You broke my trust."

"Have you got any idea what the hell you did? When I was with you in the hotel room, I've never allowed you even to touch my hand. I did mistake to trust you," she added.

Tom shrieked, "Yes! I said that, and I'm not guilty for my words. Please just once accept that you were with Edward in January."

Rose disconnected the phone. She couldn't explain herself any more.

Oh, God, in the beginning itself, I explained all to him. I agreed to his proposal just a month before, and he not even bother to clarify, Rose asked herself.

"I think this man is psycho!" Payton said.

"Oh shit! I forgot to share one thing with you. Once, he shared with me. He consulted a psychiatrist. Damn skeptical man," Rose entreated.

"How can you say that?"

"Many times, he had taken out the call records of my cell number using his contact in the companies. No articulate when I use to travel with you. He asked me many times to hear your voice to him just to check if I'm with a girl or boy."

"It means you were with the mental person until now. Thank God you escaped early."

"Yes, I evoked his previous relation also broke up because he didn't trust his fiancée. One of his friends informed him that his lover was with him on a weekend night. That's it. He never confirmed it with his fiancée and left her while she was expecting."

"It means you need to stay away from him also. He can go beyond any limits. He is dangerous," Payton warned.

"Yes, I do and I will," Rose promised.

Two years later . . .

Rose got a new job. She no longer entertained her ex-lovers after that. In this long time, she had never taken interest to know her past relations. She changed her accommodations, job, and city to stay away from her past life. Her friend Payton was still with her, supporting in each endeavor.

Family members didn't know her past life, but they suspected now also. Anglie got married to the person she loved. Rose was pleased at least her elder sister met with the love of her life.

Rose's family members had showed many options to Rose for marriage, but she did not bother to look at the photographs.

Sad memories of her past love had made her rigid, bankrupted with feelings. For a change, she tried in the airlines again, but there were no hopes alive; time had gone.

She kept on getting Tom's mail regularly every month.

He moved to a new city in search of his identity. He was a well-established business tycoon, but after coming in touch with Rose, he was captivated to build an identity and was itinerant in search of fame.

He didn't need money earlier as well as at the present, but the inferiority complex compared to Rose killed him many times. Though Rose wasn't in favor of his glamorous carrier, he still continued with that. Rose wanted to spend time with him and was glad for whatever he was, but he couldn't apprehend it.

His family members and his younger brother also convinced him not to move out from his native town, leaving business, but he hardly heeded anyone.

Finally, he handed over his entire business to his younger brother. Tom still kept waiting for Rose.

He mentioned in his mails, "If you're in my destiny, one day I'll get you."

However, she never took any action. Her first love, Edward, had left the city. He had been transferred and was promoted as well. He no longer mailed or texted her. Through the social network, she came to know . . .

"Edward got married three months ago to a beautiful girl of his ethnicity."

"What was lacking in me that he didn't marry me?" she asked God after the news.

"Rose, I request you please forget him. He was never yours. You're perfect, but you chose the wrong person," Payton said.

Rose couldn't get in as an airhostess till the time she completed her graduation. Because of her love life, she failed in her graduation exams. She would be applying for it next year if she could pass in graduation. There were still a few hopes alive.